# WE WILL FIGHT IN THE STARS

*Tales of the 142nd Starborne*

## PATRICK THOMAS

PADWOLF PUBLISHING

PADWOLF PUBLISHING INC.
WWW.PADWOLF.COM
www.facebook.com/Padwolf

www.patthomas.net

WE WILL FIGHT IN THE STARS
*Tales of the 142nd Starborne*



edited by John L. French

cover art by Patrick Thomas

cover design Roy Mauritsen and Patrick Thomas

142nd Starborne logo Mike McPhail

BETWEEN SCYLLA AND CHARYBDIS *was originally published in If We Had Known, edited by Mike McPhail*

DIVINING EVEREST *was originally published in Space Horrors, edited by David Lee Summers*

THE MACHINE IN THE GHOST *was originally published in Man and Machine, edited by Mike McPhail*

STRAY SHOT *was originally published in Dogs of War, edited by Mike McPhail*



ISBN 978-1-958310-01-4

First Printing. Printed in the USA

*For Mike McPhail
for giving me the opportunity
to create the 142$^{nd}$ Starborne*

A captain at a mobile command post signed Benedict to join her. "We've made contact, Major Benedict. They have taken the entire daycare center hostage. They're saying if the humans do not rise up and kill the vampires, all the children will die."

"Son of a corpse eater. I'm going in there," said Benedict.

"Sir, that's not exactly a good idea," said Juma. "That way not only will they have the children as hostages, but they will have you."

"The entire 142$^{nd}$ knows my policy on hostages. We do everything possible to get them out, but we do not give into demands. If anything happens to me, Morales will do an exemplary job leading the 142$^{nd}$ Starborne. I am the only one that has a chance of ending this without bloodshed." He handed off his rifle and sidearm to the colonel and turned to the captain. "Monitor my frequency. I assume snipers are already in place?"

"Yes sir. Unfortunately, he has blocked off all the windows and has space heaters going to confuse infrared."

Benedict nodded. "I will have all the communications gear that is in my uniform on full sensor mode. That should be able to get them a pretty good picture of what is inside. Have them standing by with armor-piercing shells. They will be able to tell me apart from anybody else over three feet tall. The children are *not* acceptable losses. Is that understood?"

"Yes, sir."

Benedict spoke into his headset microphone. "Tie me into the Harpies' speaker systems." Benedict heard the squelch of the feedback. "Voice, this is Benedict. I'm coming in, I'm alone and I'm unarmed."

# BOOKS BY PATRICK THOMAS

*THE MURPHY'S LORE˜ SERIES*
TALES FROM BULFINCHE'S PUB
FOOLS' DAY
THROUGH THE DRINKING GLASS
SHADOW OF THE WOLF
REDEMPTION ROAD
BARTENDER OF THE GODS
NIGHTCAPS
EMPTY GRAVES
THE MUG LIFE

*MURPHY'S LORE STARTENDERS˜*
STARTENDERS
CONSTELLATION PRIZE

*MURPHY'S LORE AFTER HOURS˜ UNIVERSE:*
**TERRORBELLE:**
FAIRY WITH A GUN
FAIRY RIDES THE LIGHTNING
TERRORBELLE THE UNCONQUERED
**AGENT KARVER:**
RITES OF PASSAGE *(with John French)*
DEAD TO RITES
**HELL'S DETECTIVE:**
LORE & DYSORDER
BULLETS & BRIMSTONE
*(with John French)*
THE CASE OF THE MOON MANIAC
*(graphic novel with Blair Webb)*
**HEXCRAFT:**
BY DARKNESS CURSED
BY INVOCATION ONLY
**SOUL FOR HIRE:**
GREATEST HITS

**XILES:**
EXILE & ENTRANCE

*BIKINI JONES:*
BIKINI JONES VS. THE
BRAINNAPPERS FROM OUT SPACE
BIKINI JONES VS THE SEA MONSTERS
BIKINI JONES VS THE EMPEROR OF
PLANET Z

**THE JACK GARDNER MYSTERIES**
THE ASSASSAINS' BALL *(with John L. French)*

**GRIFEIN, BATSQUATCH, & DINGBAT:**
CRYPTID FIGHT CLUB

**PLAYWORLDS:**
AS THE GEARS TURN:
*Tales of Steamworld*

*DEAR CTHULHU˜ SERIES*
HAVE A DARK DAY
GOOD ADVICE FOR BAD PEOPLE
CTHULHU KNOWS BEST
WHAT WOULD CTHULHU DO?
CTHULHU HAPPENS
CTHULHU EXPLAINS IT ALL
CTHULHU TAKE THE WHEEL
*MYSTIC INVESTIGATORS˜ SERIES*
MYSTIC INVESTIGATORS
MEAN STREETS
ONCE MORE IN CRIME omnibus
*by Patrick Thomas & Diane Raetz*
SHADOWS & BRIMSTONES omnibus
*by Patrick Thomas & John L. French*

**AGENTS OF THE ABYSS:**
FRANKENSTEIN: MONSTERS OF
THE ABYSS *(with John L. French)*
STARING INTO THE ABYSS: *Editor*
DETECTIVES OF THE ABYSS *(with
John L. French)*

**YA:**
THE WILDSIDHE CHRONICLES OMNIBUS
*(contributing author)*

**ANTHOLOGIES AS CO-EDITOR**
NEW BLOOD *(with Diane Raetz)*
CAMELOT 13 *(with John L. French)*

**WRITING AS PATRICK T. FIBBS**
**YA**
EMOTIONAL SUPPORT NIGHTMARE

**MIDDLE READERS:**
*UNDEAD KID DIARIES˜:*
OVER MY DEAD BODY
IT'S MY PARTY AND I'LL DIE IF I
WANT TO
*BABE B. BEAR MYSTERIES˜:*
BAD HAIR DAY
AIN'T SEEN MUFFIN YET
JOY REAPER CHECKS OUT
**YOUNGER READERS:**
*Ughaboos˜ picture books*
5 SILLY MONSTERS JUMPING
ON POOR ZED
ON TOP OF A YETI
SOGGY GOES TO THE BEACH
*an Ughaboos˜ early reader*
FUSCHIA: THE MERMAID WHO
LOVED PINK

# CONTENTS

A captain at a mobile command post signed Benedict to join her. "We've made contact, Major Benedict. They have taken the entire daycare center hostage. They're saying if the humans do not rise up and kill the vampires, all the children will die."

"Son of a corpse eater. I'm going in there," said Benedict.

"Sir, that's not exactly a good idea," said Juma. "That way not only will they have the children as hostages, but they will have you."

"The entire 142$^{nd}$ knows my policy on hostages. We do everything possible to get them out, but we do not give into demands. If anything happens to me, Morales will do an exemplary job leading the 142$^{nd}$ Starborne. I am the only one that has a chance of ending this without bloodshed." He handed off his rifle and sidearm to the colonel and turned to the captain. "Monitor my frequency. I assume snipers are already in place?"

"Yes sir. Unfortunately, he has blocked off all the windows and has space heaters going to confuse infrared."

Benedict nodded. "I will have all the communications gear that is in my uniform on full sensor mode. That should be able to get them a pretty good picture of what is inside. Have them standing by with armor-piercing shells. They will be able to tell me apart from anybody else over three feet tall. The children are *not* acceptable losses. Is that understood?"

"Yes, sir."

Benedict spoke into his headset microphone. "Tie me into the Harpies' speaker systems." Benedict heard the squelch of the feedback. "Voice, this is Benedict. I'm coming in, I'm alone and I'm unarmed."

# BOOKS BY PATRICK THOMAS

***The Murphy's Lore™ series***
TALES FROM BULFINCHE'S PUB
FOOLS' DAY
THROUGH THE DRINKING GLASS
SHADOW OF THE WOLF
REDEMPTION ROAD
BARTENDER OF THE GODS
NIGHTCAPS
EMPTY GRAVES
THE MUG LIFE

***Murphy's Lore Startenders™***
STARTENDERS
CONSTELLATION PRIZE

***Murphy's Lore After Hours™ Universe:***
**Terrorbelle:**
FAIRY WITH A GUN
FAIRY RIDES THE LIGHTNING
TERRORBELLE THE UNCONQUERED
 **Agent Karver:**
RITES OF PASSAGE *(with John French)*
DEAD TO RITES
**Hell's Detective:**
LORE & DYSORDER
BULLETS & BRIMSTONE
 *(with John French)*
THE CASE OF THE MOON MANIAC
 *(graphic novel with Blair Webb)*
**Hexcraft:**
BY DARKNESS CURSED
BY INVOCATION ONLY
**Soul for Hire:**
GREATEST HITS

**Xiles:**
EXILE & ENTRANCE

***Bikini Jones:***
BIKINI JONES VS. THE
BRAINNAPPERS FROM OUT SPACE
BIKINI JONES VS THE SEA MONSTERS
BIKINI JONES VS THE EMPEROR OF
PLANET Z

**THE JACK GARDNER MYSTERIES**
THE ASSASSAINS' BALL *(with John L. French)*

**Grifein, Batsquatch, & Dingbat:**
CRYPTID FIGHT CLUB

**Playworlds:**
AS THE GEARS TURN:
 *Tales of Steamworld*

***Dear Cthulhu™ Series***
HAVE A DARK DAY
GOOD ADVICE FOR BAD PEOPLE
CTHULHU KNOWS BEST
WHAT WOULD CTHULHU DO?
CTHULHU HAPPENS
CTHULHU EXPLAINS IT ALL
CTHULHU TAKE THE WHEEL
***Mystic Investigators™ series***
MYSTIC INVESTIGATORS
MEAN STREETS
ONCE MORE IN CRIME omnibus
 *by Patrick Thomas & Diane Raetz*
SHADOWS & BRIMSTONES omnibus
 *by Patrick Thomas & John L. French*

***Agents of the Abyss:***
FRANKENSTEIN: MONSTERS OF
THE ABYSS *(with John L. French)*
STARING INTO THE ABYSS: *Editor*
DETECTIVES OF THE ABYSS *(with
John L. French)*

**YA:**
THE WILDSIDHE CHRONICLES OMNIBUS
*(contributing author)*

**Anthologies as co-editor**
NEW BLOOD *(with Diane Raetz)*
CAMELOT 13 *(with John L. French)*

**Writing as Patrick T. Fibbs**
**ya**
EMOTIONAL SUPPORT NIGHTMARE

**MIDDLE READERS:**
*UNDEAD KID DIARIES™:*
 OVER MY DEAD BODY
 IT'S MY PARTY AND I'LL DIE IF I
WANT TO
*BABE B. BEAR MYSTERIES™:*
 BAD HAIR DAY
 AIN'T SEEN MUFFIN YET
JOY REAPER CHECKS OUT
**YOUNGER READERS:**
*Ughaboos™ picture books*
 5 SILLY MONSTERS JUMPING
 ON POOR ZED
ON TOP OF A YETI
*SOGGY GOES TO THE BEACH*
 *an Ughaboos™ early reader*
FUSCHIA: THE MERMAID WHO
 LOVED PINK

A captain at a mobile command post signed Benedict to join her. "We've made contact, Major Benedict. They have taken the entire daycare center hostage. They're saying if the humans do not rise up and kill the vampires, all the children will die."

"Son of a corpse eater. I'm going in there," said Benedict.

"Sir, that's not exactly a good idea," said Juma. "That way not only will they have the children as hostages, but they will have you."

"The entire 142$^{nd}$ knows my policy on hostages. We do everything possible to get them out, but we do not give into demands. If anything happens to me, Morales will do an exemplary job leading the 142$^{nd}$ Starborne. I am the only one that has a chance of ending this without bloodshed." He handed off his rifle and sidearm to the colonel and turned to the captain. "Monitor my frequency. I assume snipers are already in place?"

"Yes sir. Unfortunately, he has blocked off all the windows and has space heaters going to confuse infrared."

Benedict nodded. "I will have all the communications gear that is in my uniform on full sensor mode. That should be able to get them a pretty good picture of what is inside. Have them standing by with armor-piercing shells. They will be able to tell me apart from anybody else over three feet tall. The children are *not* acceptable losses. Is that understood?"

"Yes, sir."

Benedict spoke into his headset microphone. "Tie me into the Harpies' speaker systems." Benedict heard the squelch of the feedback. "Voice, this is Benedict. I'm coming in, I'm alone and I'm unarmed."

# BOOKS BY PATRICK THOMAS

*THE MURPHY'S LORE™ SERIES*
TALES FROM BULFINCHE'S PUB
FOOLS' DAY
THROUGH THE DRINKING GLASS
SHADOW OF THE WOLF
REDEMPTION ROAD
BARTENDER OF THE GODS
NIGHTCAPS
EMPTY GRAVES
THE MUG LIFE

*MURPHY'S LORE STARTENDERS™*
STARTENDERS
CONSTELLATION PRIZE

*MURPHY'S LORE AFTER HOURS™ UNIVERSE:*
**TERRORBELLE:**
FAIRY WITH A GUN
FAIRY RIDES THE LIGHTNING
TERRORBELLE THE UNCONQUERED
**AGENT KARVER:**
RITES OF PASSAGE *(with John French)*
DEAD TO RITES
**HELL'S DETECTIVE:**
LORE & DYSORDER
BULLETS & BRIMSTONE
*(with John French)*
THE CASE OF THE MOON MANIAC
*(graphic novel with Blair Webb)*
**HEXCRAFT:**
BY DARKNESS CURSED
BY INVOCATION ONLY
**SOUL FOR HIRE:**
GREATEST HITS

**XILES:**
EXILE & ENTRANCE

*BIKINI JONES:*
BIKINI JONES VS. THE
BRAINNAPPERS FROM OUT SPACE
BIKINI JONES VS THE SEA MONSTERS
BIKINI JONES VS THE EMPEROR OF
PLANET Z

**THE JACK GARDNER MYSTERIES**
THE ASSASSAINS' BALL *(with John L. French)*

**GRIFEIN, BATSQUATCH, & DINGBAT:**
CRYPTID FIGHT CLUB

**PLAYWORLDS:**
AS THE GEARS TURN:
*Tales of Steamworld*

*DEAR CTHULHU™ SERIES*
HAVE A DARK DAY
GOOD ADVICE FOR BAD PEOPLE
CTHULHU KNOWS BEST
WHAT WOULD CTHULHU DO?
CTHULHU HAPPENS
CTHULHU EXPLAINS IT ALL
CTHULHU TAKE THE WHEEL
*MYSTIC INVESTIGATORS™ SERIES*
MYSTIC INVESTIGATORS
MEAN STREETS
ONCE MORE IN CRIME omnibus
*by Patrick Thomas & Diane Raetz*
SHADOWS & BRIMSTONES omnibus
*by Patrick Thomas & John L. French*

*AGENTS OF THE ABYSS:*
FRANKENSTEIN: MONSTERS OF
THE ABYSS *(with John L. French)*
STARING INTO THE ABYSS: *Editor*
DETECTIVES OF THE ABYSS *(with
John L. French)*

**YA:**
THE WILDSIDHE CHRONICLES OMNIBUS
*(contributing author)*

**ANTHOLOGIES AS CO-EDITOR**
NEW BLOOD *(with Diane Raetz)*
CAMELOT 13 *(with John L. French)*

**WRITING AS PATRICK T. FIBBS**
**YA**
EMOTIONAL SUPPORT NIGHTMARE

**MIDDLE READERS:**
*UNDEAD KID DIARIES™:*
OVER MY DEAD BODY
IT'S MY PARTY AND I'LL DIE IF I
WANT TO
*BABE B. BEAR MYSTERIES™:*
BAD HAIR DAY
AIN'T SEEN MUFFIN YET
JOY REAPER CHECKS OUT
**YOUNGER READERS:**
*Ughaboos™ picture books*
5 SILLY MONSTERS JUMPING
ON POOR ZED
ON TOP OF A YETI
SOGGY GOES TO THE BEACH
*an Ughaboos™ early reader*
FUSCHIA: THE MERMAID WHO
LOVED PINK

# BETWEEN SCYLLA AND CHARYBDIS

Major Hans Benedict watched the alien vessel approach, from the point it first appeared as a dot in the distance, until it was finally close enough to block everything else from his sight.

It was time to get to work.

Waiting had been the easy part. The next step was tricky. The ship they dubbed *Magog* had ignored all attempts to communicate as it headed directly for the human settlement on Kailash. As it came closer, it dissolved any drones and satellites it encountered into their component atoms. Approaching it, even in something designed to look like space debris, didn't seem like a good idea. Which is why, as the best sapper in the 142$^{nd}$ Starborne, Benedict got the job. The fact that his superior officer General Daily believed it was a suicide mission didn't matter. Hans Benedict had never shirked his duty or disobeyed an order, not even when he fully expected to be vaporized into a cloud of atoms.

*Behemoth's* long-range sensors could not penetrate *Magog's* hull but had located what was assumed to be a clear viewport midway up the ship. Most Host warships limited viewports because of the risk of a hull breach, but they had several as a backup in case their sensors failed. For a ship the size of a large asteroid, it seemed odd to have only one, but Benedict was thankful for it. Otherwise, he wouldn't have a decent point of entry, assuming he lived long enough to make the attempt.

That single window was the target at which Benedict had launched his coffin, which is not as easy as it sounds. A coffin was basically just that—a sealed cylinder with windows, a minimal amount of air, and only an old-fashioned, hand-cranked radio for communications. No other technology to be picked up by the target's sensors. Multiple liners to mask any life signs.

Not only did he have to figure his own trajectory, but that of the *Magog*, calculate where and when the two would meet, and then wait. It was akin to shooting at a target that was out of range, then getting the bullet to stop and wait for the target to run into the bullet hours later. It was risky. One small miscalculation would ensure that the gargantuan ship smashed him and his coffin to pieces, assuming he didn't get atomized first.

As soon as he was inside the range at which the earlier probes were disintegrated, he found himself gritting his teeth, waiting to be destroyed.

Benedict almost missed the target, but only almost. He had planned for his coffin to land in the middle of the lone window, but he missed that mark. Half of his coffin was on the hull and the other half on the window. The coffin's hull had nodules that burst upon impact to release a thick paste that worked as a shock absorber and quickly hardened to adhere it to the alien ship.

It worked. Clad in a black spacesuit, Benedict emerged from the coffin and headed toward the window. He looked inside, wondering if all his planning would be ruined by someone inside looking out at space. Fortunately, the room was empty. Quickly, he used a molecular cutter to carve a hole big enough for him to board the ship. Instead of glass or plastic, the window itself was made out of some sort of crystalline substance two feet thick. It was almost half an hour later when he pushed the cut section in and moved to the side as the chunk of window was shot outward by escaping gasses. Using specially designed boots and gloves, he managed to pull himself inside. Benedict quickly spun and placed a breach patch over his work. It wouldn't go unnoticed during a visual examination, but it did stop more of whatever passed for atmosphere in the ship from being lost to the vacuum.

After checking his patchwork, Benedict crouched down and remained still as he assessed his surroundings. The atmosphere was remarkably similar to that of Earth, with lower nitrogen and higher oxygen and argon levels. Like *Behemoth*, the *Magog* had artificial gravity, although about ten percent higher than Earth normal.

Host ships had corridors and rooms built from pieces placed together in rectangular formations, but the alien ship, or at least the room he'd entered, appeared to lack seams. The surface was covered with ridges and bumps similar to those formed by painting with a sponge.

Most importantly, Benedict saw no signs of life or any form of mechanical detection. He had hoped he wouldn't find any. Not just to make his job easier, but because of his orders. If the ship was abandoned, the Host would take it as salvage and learn as much as it could about its technology. However, if the ship was not running on automated sensors and had a crew, standard orders from the Sway government back on Earth were clear. Kill them all.

Almost two centuries may have passed since the Earth was first invaded, but those in power hadn't forgotten that the planet had only been saved by a fluke set of circumstances and the insight of one man, the same man who later would unite the planet under the Sway government. Their directive was clear. Any alien races or cultures encountered that appeared to have a higher technology level than the Sway must be destroyed in a show of force so as to discourage any thought of an attack on Earth or one of the colony worlds.

Benedict was a good soldier. He would follow orders then deal with the wounds to his conscience later.

His guess that he was in an observation room seemed correct. There were lumps lining the floor, walls, and ceilings that might have been seats, as if whatever used them were not restricted to the floor. Maybe gravity for this room could be turned off.

Exiting the room was a problem. His examination of the room gave him the impression that it had been molded rather than assembled. There were no panels or tiles to open and no visible exit. Walking clockwise around the room, closely examining the walls Benedict eventually found a coin-sized area that could be pressed down. Hoping it wasn't a some sort of communication device, he did so, heard a click, and saw a circular opening appear in the wall, one that led to a corridor.

The corridor was cylindrical, with no flat surface to walk on. It took several steps for Benedict to adapt to walking on the curved surface. Like the observation room, the corridor had no noticeable seams. Scanners attached to his chest, back, and wrists took readings on everything, feeding the data to a contact in his left eye.

The *Magog* may have been resistant to *Behemoth's* external scanners, but now that he was inside he was able to detect several energy signatures, including one that was giving off enough juice to power a medium-sized city, but with no harmful radiation. If the Host could figure out how the ship was putting out that level of power, it might be a new energy source for all the colony worlds, making life for the settlers that much easier.

Through trial and error, Benedict started to recognize the slightly different impressions that indicated where the doors were. Each had a camouflaged disc that popped up when you pressed it. The switch had a hole in the center. Benedict needed to stick his finger in and turn counterclockwise as he pulled to open the doors. The rest of the corridor doors were different than the first he encountered and were brilliant pieces of engineering. A circular portion of a wall opened as sections of the wall separated into individual rods that pointed from the outside toward an empty space in the center. The nearby parts of the doors wound around the rods, not unlike an old-fashioned blind. They were not easy to walk through without being poked or jabbed, so Benedict got in the habit of holding onto two of the upper rods to lift himself up and swing through feet first.

Two hours later, as he approached the energy signal, he still had not come across any living beings or automations. The ship seemed in perfect working order, so it made no sense for its makers to have abandoned it.

When he turned the last open switch, a larger circular section of wall simply disappeared like in the observation room.

The second thing he noticed was the dead alien at his feet. The first was the individual tube-like vertical chambers that stretched on for what looked like miles. Each had a view port made from the same crystalline structure as the hull window, allowing him to see inside. And each contained the body of what he could only assume were members of the race that made the ship.

They were not humanoid.

Benedict's first impression was that the race that had built the *Magog* was storing some kind of seafood, at least judging by the appearance of the creatures, which appeared to be some sort of variation on the octopus or squid. Closer examination revealed significant differences. These creatures had ten tentacles, six serving as what he thought of as legs and four that might be considered arms. No fingers, no opposable digits, but what looked like an alternating mixture of suckers and single claws.

It was hard to tell for sure, but they looked like they had five of what passed for eyes spread over the front and sides of what was likely the head. He couldn't make out ears, a nose, or a mouth. The creatures were long, and wide at the bottom like a bulbous umbrella.

For a civilization to make the effort to put this many of their people on a ship this advanced, there should have been some sort of internal defense or at least guards. Benedict kept waiting for an attack that never came.

As he continued his exploration of the bio-storage facility, he came across the likely reason for his lack of a reception. At least twenty of the creatures lay spread across the floor, dead and decaying, their purple flesh sloughing off their bones. Although bones might not have been the right term. Their skeletons looked thin and flexible, more like cartilage. Each alien corpse had holes cut clean through their bodies, but no incineration or energy burns. It was as if parts of their bodies had just ceased to be.

Still clad in his spacesuit, Benedict bent down to remove something from one of the dead creature's arm tentacles. It looked like a long, thick metal cylinder that had been sliced in half the long way. It had two bands that connected it to the tentacle and ended in a point. Each of the dead—Benedict decided to call them Magogians—wore two, each with slightly different markings and shades. They each gave off unfamiliar, yet distinct energy signatures.

Benedict assumed they were weapons and he took several moments figuring out how they were triggered. The two holding rings that connected it to the tentacle had sensors. The Magogians must have been able to flex segments of their tentacles to press on both sensors at the same time. Benedict theorized that hitting them both at the same time would fire the weapon. It was dangerous and stupid to attempt, but he had to assume that whoever shot them was still alive and would come across him eventually. Without knowing their exact physiology, he could not be certain his sidearm would kill a Magogian, but these things likely could.

Holding the first weapon with the point out, the same way he found it on the tentacle, Benedict experimented. By hitting the closer sensor first, then the further one, it let out a glowing mist that seemed to ride on a beam of energy. He pointed it at one of the dead Magogians and pressed the sensors. The creature's flesh dissolved into a mist which then vanished, much like what had happened to the Host's probes. Extending the time between pressing the sensors built up a more powerful charge that made hunks of metal go away.

He picked up the second weapon. It was of a similar shape, but shorter and made of a darker metal. It had the same triggering sensors. He pointed it toward the floor and fired. A beam of energy shot out that melted the surface of the tubular deck.

Benedict let out a short, surprised whistle. While the Host had energy weapons, they were mounted on ships because they hadn't been able to miniaturize them enough for a soldier to carry safely. The Magogians had obviously figured out how to make it work.

His contact lens screen flared to life and Benedict closed his left eye to see it better. There was a power surge not far from his location. He rushed to investigate, taking the energy weapons with him.

At the center of the surge, there was a living, moving Magogian standing in front of rows of glowing extrusions.

Benedict had his orders. He stepped out, planning to shoot the creature with the energy weapon, when the machine hummed and the glow suddenly expanded, enveloping both Benedict and the Magogian in a glittering nimbus.

The ship was gone. Benedict stood above a blue, living planet as the history of that world unfolded before him. He watched as the Magogians left their oceans, rose and fell, built civilizations, created art, made love and war, and developed space travel. They went out to explore the universe but did not colonize, choosing instead to learn. On one excursion, their ship discovered a dead world. Scientists gathered artifacts and brought them back to their world, which they referred to in their own language simply as "Home," just as they referred to themselves as "Us."

They set about trying to deduce what had destroyed the world they found. The idea of a planetary apocalypse disturbed them so much that they set about building space arks, a way to make sure their race would survive even if Home did not.

It took years for them to complete the first ark and they

had begun work on the second when tragedy struck. Their scholars had continued examining artifacts from the dead world and opened a book the scanners showed was bound with organic material, most likely some sort of dermis or skin.

The scholars tried to open their minds in hopes of deciphering what was written. One succeeded, then made the mistake of reading the text aloud.

Benedict watched in horror as the book opened a portal to a place of unspeakable darkness. Nightmares came through to destroy Home. The only good fortune was that the completed ark lay on the other side of the world. Many Us—Benedict decided to change what he called them to Usian—panicked, but others came up with a plan. They could not stop the aliens, but they were able to slow their progress. Tens of millions, maybe more, brave Usians did not hide or try to save themselves. Instead, they fought against the nightmares destroying Home in an effort to hold back the dark invaders long enough for the ark to be filled with one million of their people and launched into space.

And through sheer determination, they succeeded. The ark now searched for a new home and its sensors had located a suitable world. The Us were essentially a compassionate people, so Benedict assumed they hadn't realized that Kailash was already inhabited by a human settlement or they would have kept looking. Explanations of the ship, its systems, the weapons, Usian biology, and even languages were downloaded into Benedict's mind.

He now knew how to maintain the status tubes, pilot the ship, and even some basic medical care for the Usians.

Then the images vanished and he was left feeling dizzy and, for a moment, like he had too few limbs.

The teachings he had absorbed had been comforting and made him forget for a moment where he was and what he was doing. The Usian who had triggered the knowledge device recovered faster and realized the human was behind him and lashed out with a rapid-fire blur of tentacles that stripped him of the energy weapon and knocked him, battered and bruised, to the deck.

The creature screamed at him with sounds that should have been incomprehensible to the human but weren't.

"What be you and why you be here?" the creature demanded.

Benedict struggled with his vocal chords and tried to mimic the sounds needed to answer as he got to his feet and tried to back out of tentacle reach.

"Me Major Hans Benedict…" His name and rank were said in English as there was no equivalent and the Usians had a different grammar structure. "…of the Host. Us ship is approaching We world. Please reverse course, leave system."

"World holds no true civilization."

"We have settlement."

"Barely any."

"One hundred thousand."

The creature trilled like a bird going through a food processor. It was a laugh.

"Over one million Us ride ark. Need ours greater than need yours."

Benedict knew the Usians to be a determined people and the ark unable to achieve orbit again once it landed on a planet. The Usians would claim Kailash, likely the same spot the human settlement had, as it was the most hospitable to both races. Most Usians would offer to let the humans leave, but Benedict knew the human settlers would fight to the death before giving up the world they were making their own. Now that it was found that the ship was not abandoned, standing orders demanded that Benedict destroy the Usians and their ark.

For the first time in his career, Benedict hesitated. Having experienced what it was like to be one of the Usians, even for a moment, left him loath to commit what amounted to genocide.

In desperation, Benedict tried logic. "Us hold lives blessed. Against slaughter."

The Usian laughed again. "Honor Protectors prattle same fools' speak. Want Us leave system to find another world to settle. Me old, fatigued from so many time wasted in search. World become ours. Me kill rest Protectors. Learner beam teach Me flying of ship. Land then awake rest Us. Will send to atoms others on world so Me finally rest."

"Lives be ended."

"Lives be restarted. Time for others to pass beyond, starting on you."

Responding to the death threat, Benedict pulled out his sidearm and fired at the Usain's center eye as he fled. He hit his fleshy target, barely slowing the mass of angry tentacles which sped after him, using the walls and ceilings instead of the floor.

The creature shot an energy beam and would have hit Benedict had he not zigged to the side, running full out toward the nearest status tubes. Once inside the large chamber, his tentacled attacker no longer had the high ground advantage, as the chamber was too enormous and the walls too far away from where Benedict ran. He fired at the Usian, wasting shots that did the tentapod little harm until he ran out of ammunition.

The major scanned for weapons and found none. Benedict crouched to get his bearings behind a status pod, thinking himself safe, for the only way to shoot him now would be to take out another one of the Usians.

An energy beam cut through the pod and its occupant, missing Benedict's head by inches.

The alien was beyond reason, willing to kill its own people to get at the sapper.

Running behind the chambers, Benedict headed back toward the nearest pile of bodies, energy beams destroying pods all around him.

He ran by an alien corpse, grabbed hold of the nearest weapon — one of the lighter, metal variety—and kept moving. The tentacle tore off, so Benedict pulled it out of the rings and put his index fingers near the sensors and pressed the rear one. Aiming forward of where he estimated the last energy beam came from, he dove to the ground and hit the forward sensor, sending a dissolving beam of light and mist out.

Benedict kept moving. He assumed he hadn't hit his target or there would have been screaming.

Where the hell was that tentacled bastard?

He heard a clang and fired in that direction, realizing too late it was a ploy, the noise likely coming from something his opponent threw as a distraction.

Something grabbed his ankle, pulling him down and out from behind the pods. A second tentacle reached out and pulled something off the alien weapon in his hand. Benedict fired at point-blank range but nothing happened.

The Usian jiggled a metal piece from the hook on the end of his tentacle. "No power no work."

Another tentacle wrapped around Benedict's neck and

lifted him off of the floor and into the air so his face and what passed for the alien's head lined up.

The alien laughed, then stopped as Benedict rammed the pointed end of the weapon through the fleshly area that would be a human's neck, but he now knew housed the alien's motor cortex. The medical training the beam had taught him had included what areas were most important to stabilize in the event of injury. Which meant that those areas also made the best kill points. The alien murderer stiffened before sliding to the ground, its tentacle still wrapped around Benedict's throat.

Benedict pulled the limb off, gasping for air. "Still works pretty good I'd say."

He slid the combat knife off his belt and quickly stabbed several more vital areas to make sure the creature was truly dead.

He returned to his coffin to retrieve the explosives he had brought with him and spent the next ten hours placing them around the ship in what the learning beam had shown him were the ship's most vital systems. Now having intimate knowledge of how their communications array worked, he could launch his coffin, radio for pick up, and detonate them remotely.

But these people were the last of their race. Slaughtering them while they slept in status was the act of a monster, not a soldier. Genocide was too horrible to contemplate but if the Usians awoke and tried to take Kailash, even *Behemoth* couldn't stand against their energy weapons for long.

There had to be another option. A way to get the Usians out of the system and away from human settlements and have the general and the Host believe that the ship had been destroyed.

Benedict returned to the learning beam. Thanks to his prior exposure, he not only knew how to activate it, but how to have it teach him specific things. He needed to know about the status chambers and how the ship traveled between star systems.

A plan slowly came to him. He reprogrammed the ship, then evacuated via the coffin as the ship reversed course. It was quickly out of weapons range.

"Sapper One needs pickup," he said after cranking up the radio.

"Roger that, Sapper One. Harpy dropship Beta Four is *en route* to your location."

A short while later Benedict was sitting in the dropship's cockpit with General Dailey on the view screen.

It was Major Hans Benedict's educated and personal judgment that General Dailey was a five-star idiot. Not that as a career man the major would ever repeat those thoughts aloud to anyone.

"Well, Major, what's the story? Is the ship salvage or a target?"

"Target, sir."

"Then why is it intact? And moving away from us?"

"I wanted a larger perimeter for safety."

"Why?"

As if in answer, there was an EMP burst, followed by the ship's disintegration weapons discharging a luminescent cloud instead of a beam.

A moment later the ship was gone.

Dailey's mouth fell open. "You reduced the entire ship to atoms? How?"

"It wasn't easy, turning the ship upon itself." Or at least giving the appearance of doing so. The electromagnetic pulse helped disguise the ship exiting the system. Benedict gambled that since the *Behemoth's* sensors didn't detect it until after it arrived in the system, the same would be true of *Magog's* exit. It was on its way to a system far down the Sway government's list for colonization. There were currently three hundred worlds approved for consideration and fifty more that were suitable, but not ideal. He chose the best one off the second list that was on the outskirts of mapped space as it would not likely be colonized for at least a century, if at all.

The status chambers would open one hundred pods as they entered that system and those hundred Usians would be enough to prepare the rest of the ship for planet fall.

Benedict planned to file a report that he had information that this system was likely inhabited and have it delivered to the Host High Command after his death to prevent any surprises for future colonists. The Usians would be cannibalizing the *Magog* to rebuild themselves and would no longer be a space-faring threat and thus the standing order to destroy them would not apply.

"You are confident that the *Magog* is no longer a threat to humanity?"

"I am, General." And he was. Major Hans Benedict was no one's fool. He was aware that something could happen and the ship might even return, but he had erased the *Magog's* sensor sweeps from the period that he planted the bombs and all records of their time in the Indus system. Should the need arise, he could cripple or destroy the ship remotely.

He hoped it wouldn't because his career would be over. But disobeying orders to save one million lives—the remains of an entire race and civilization—was the right thing to do. The honorable path to take. The only path for a soldier to take.

"Meet me in command for a full debriefing as soon as you are back on *Behemoth*."

"Yes, sir."

As he disembarked the Harpy, he tripped and the pilot had to catch him.

"Careful, Major. Breaking in new feet?"

For a moment, Benedict's mind had been trying to walk with six tentacles instead of legs, causing him to trip.

"No, Captain. Breaking in the old ones."

# A SOLDIER'S DUTY

ajor Hans Benedict had often stared into the face of stupidity but never with so much at stake. "But sir, Diamondhead is facing a planetwide extinction event."

"So is Earth."

Major Hans Benedict frowned then forced himself to stop. General Dailey was a five-star idiot but even he couldn't possibly be about to suggest a pointless suicide mission. "With all due respect General, Earth *faced* an extinction-level event and lost. Our home world is a smoldering ruin and all fifteen billion of her people lay dead."

"Not all of them, Benedict. The highest-ranking members of the Sway government managed to get to a bunker. That includes the men and women who are in charge of the Host military. As soldiers of the Host, we are obliged to follow their orders. We will break orbit from Diamondhead and make the journey back to Earth at 0600 hours."

"General, I saw the same transmission you did. Those…" After what he had seen, Benedict couldn't bring himself to call them leaders. "…high ranking officials played with nature to the point where the Sway has zombie servants and bloodsucking soldiers. They were trying to get their hands on something even more powerful and opened that maw into darkness. That *thing* came through their portal…" It was the same type of monstrosity that had destroyed the Usians. "… and slaughtered billions. Every Host ship that answered their call has been destroyed. It's insanity to risk the crew of the *Behemoth* for two hundred people who brought on the destruction of our homeworld. There are more than fifty times that number on board this ship and half a million more on the world below us. If we stop before we divert or destroy the remaining three asteroids, those half a million people below we are tasked with protecting will be dead in three days."

There was no pause for thought, no time taken for consideration. Orders were given so the orders must be followed. Daily did not get to be a general by questioning a command and he never considered it even now when any logical thinker would have. "We will go back to Earth, rescue the Sway survivors then return in time to save the population of Diamondhead."

"General, you know that's impossible. In three days' time, everyone on the planet below us will be dead. Using every resource at our command, it'll take us almost four days to get back to Earth."

"Benedict, we are soldiers of the Sway. We obey orders and we have been ordered back to protect Earth," Dailey said.

"You're right. We are soldiers of the Sway. You took the same oath that I did. We swore to protect life at the cost of our own and fight for the greater good. Those selfish people in the bunker on Earth were behind the incursion that wiped out the rest of the population. Whatever is on the *planet* can destroy ships in *space*. It's already destroyed five other Colossus-class warships. If the *Behemoth* goes back to Earth, we will be destroyed and everyone on board will die. It makes no sense to sacrifice that many lives for two hundred people who just brought about the slaughter of fifteen billion members of the human race. Sir, you are a general of the Host. Right now, you may be the highest-ranking military officer alive. You have the authority to countermand that wrongful order so we stay to save the civilians on Diamondhead. Not only do you have the authority, but you have the duty and the obligation to save those lives as per our last lawful order."

"We will leave behind a few harpies."

"You know as well as I do that dropships alone will not be able to stop those asteroids."

"Harpies already helped take out a dozen asteroids."

"All of them smaller than these three."

"Benedict, aren't you supposed to be the best sapper the Host has ever seen? Are you telling me you couldn't take care of three measly asteroids with a few dropships and some explosives?"

"Not well enough for me to can be confident about getting the job done right."

"We have our orders, Benedict. We will follow them."

"Understood, General, but there's nothing saying that we can't finish the job here first. In a little over two days, we will have diverted the two larger asteroids and destroyed the smaller one. All I'm asking is that we postpone a suicide mission long enough to save half a million innocent lives."

"Benedict, I'm not in the habit of repeating myself once, let alone this many times. The orders from the Sway are specific and were delayed only because our array has been down for days after the nukes we used on the other asteroids. There is no more time to delay."

A corporal knocked at the door of the ready room. "General, you wanted to be notified the moment all ship's personnel had returned. The entire crew is on board and accounted for."

"Thank you, Corporal. Looks like we leave for Earth

immediately." Dailey informed the bridge and *Behemoth* left Diamondhead's orbit.

Major Benedict became very pale. "Sir, the people on Diamondhead…"

"We are on our way to Earth. You said dropships wouldn't do the job, so I will not waste the resources. They are on their own. This discussion is over. Is that understood?"

"I understand your orders, just not the reasoning for it, sir."

"Your understanding matters less to me than what happened to my last bowel movement."

"Sir, please listen to what Major Benedict is saying," pleaded Captain Shana Morales.

"Don't tell me that you're afraid to engage with the enemy?" Dailey said.

"No sir, I'm not, but without a battle plan, we may as well fly *Behemoth* into Diamondhead's sun and save us all the trip to Earth. We've seen the footage. Whatever that thing is, it can survive nukes and is large enough to be seen from orbit. It and its foot soldiers are more powerful than our entire fleet. I won't shy away from a fight but throwing away lives for no chance of gain is against everything the Host stands for. What is your plan?" Morales asked.

"Right now, the Sol system's planets are lined up in a row for the first time in who knows how long. We come in system using them for cover, then we park out behind Mars. We send a couple of harpies in to do recon," Dailey said.

"Won't work, sir. We are getting a transmission from *Goliath*. They were trying to put the moon between them and whatever this thing is. Every harpy and drone they sent in was destroyed before even reaching the atmosphere. Then it turned its attention to the *Goliath*," said Colonel

Bai Zhang. The *Behemoth's* intelligence officer had been analyzing transmissions nonstop since they first got them two hours ago.

A scene of the bridge of the other Colossus-class ship was put on the main screen. The screams of the dying crew made the men and women around the table blanch and lower their eyes.

General Dailey spared a moment to turn and look at the horrors on the screen. "Get that off of there. We need to focus here."

The image vanished but Colonel Zhang kept watching the screen in front of him. He then closed his eyes and bowed his head for the briefest of moments. "The *Goliath* has been destroyed, General."

"A tragedy but one we won't repeat. When we get there, we'll send in Benedict and his sappers in a bunch of coffins and let them do recon," Dailey said.

Benedict was fighting to keep himself under control but dealing with a so-called superior officer who didn't mourn the loss of fellow soldiers or understand how to use his basic assets was infuriating. It was supposed to be a simple inspection with the General onboard for one tour of duty but, ignoring protocol, the man took over the ship a year ago which due to his five-star rank was within his prerogative.

"It won't work, General. The reason coffins are good for stealth and why they're so hard to detect is because they have no means of propulsion other than momentum. No modern electronics to be picked up by sensors. Basically, a coffin is a cylinder with air. They're meant for boarding ships and sky stations."

"I'd be okay with that if we got the intel we needed," Dailey said.

"You shouldn't be because you won't get anything. Once we hit the atmosphere, all we'd do is crash and burn. Even if we somehow made it to the surface without being cooked or crushed, you still wouldn't get any decent intel because the only transmitting device onboard is an ancient radio. Any coffin sent would be on a one-way ticket to oblivion. Sappers go on suicide missions all the time when there is a clear objective. Turning into a meteorite and dying without any other purpose is not a clear objective," Benedict said.

Dailey was just as infuriated with Benedict as the sapper was with him, only the General realized he had revealed his own ignorance to his subordinates. "Fine then, Benedict, how would you get them out get them off-world?"

"With a rescue mission like this, you need to start with either overwhelming firepower or a very good distraction. These creatures don't seem to have any weak or blind spots. We reviewed some of the footage from ships that tried entering orbit from different points around the globe and it didn't matter. They were all destroyed. The only way we can get those people out is if they were able to break orbit on their own. Then we could run in, make a grab and make a beeline out of the system," Benedict said.

The General shook his head. "The transmission was very clear. They have no access to any transportation and are trapped in the bunker. We need to clear the enemy from a quarter-mile radius around that bunker."

"Which is pretty impossible to do when we can't even get into orbit," Morales said.

"The bunker was built to withstand a nuclear blast. Why don't we send a nuke to clear the area?" said Captain Koss Wende, the General's aide.

General Dailey took a deep breath. "The Sway already

launched tactical nuclear strikes which took out New York, London, Beijing, Lagos, Rio, Tokyo, and Delhi. The effects on the smaller enemy creatures outside of the blast radius were minimal. However, once the *Behemoth* clears the moon, we could launch a repeating cascade of nukes in front of us until we get close enough to nuke the site, then launch harpies for evac."

"Following a trail of that many nukes in succession may leave more radiation behind than our shielding can handle, not to mention traveling through all those EMPs. If we did manage to get to the bunker and get them out, they'd have to go through a freshly nuked landscape. Everyone on board the rescue ship would be dead within a year from radiation poisoning," Zhang said. "And the chances of the rest of us surviving until retirement won't look good."

No one mentioned that without a central government or military authority, retirement was not going to be what it used to be.

"Fine. We need plans. We will meet back here in five hours and I want everyone to have at least two ideas of how we can get those people off Earth. Dismissed."

Morales, Zhang, and Benedict left together and convened in Zhang's office where they reviewed more of the footage the destroyed fleet had transmitted.

The fleet had had only seven Colossus-class ships other than *Behemoth*. They reviewed the footage as the *Goliath* and five others were destroyed by the thing on the surface. The seventh, the *Gargantuan* had transmitted that it was en route to Earth.

"If it wasn't for the EMPs blocking communications, that would have been us," Morales said.

"There is no way we can come up with a plan to destroy

that thing in four days." Benedict reviewed everything he had seen in the learning matrix onboard the *Maggog*. With far more advanced weapons, the Usians hadn't been able to do more than stall long enough for their ark to launch. The Host didn't have a hope. "Or maybe ever."

"I concur," Zhang said.

"So, we commit suicide to feed the General's ego?" Morales said.

"I will not allow the settlers on Diamondhead to die by asteroid," Benedict said.

"If we get the general to allow you to go back with dropships, could you stop them?" Morales said.

"The little one? Yes. The next one? Maybe. The large one? No," Benedict said. "Even if this pyrrhic mission is successful, we should not have abandoned half a million innocents to die from a shockwave or tsunamis and the ensuring planetary winter. Especially not to save a harpy-load of people who destroyed our homeworld in a bid for more power. This is not acceptable. I will not allow it to happen," Benedict said. "Not again."

"Again?"

"Again?" Zhang said.

"Allow all the people on a planet to die," Benedict covered.

"But we've already left the system," Morales said.

Benedict nodded. "I need *Behemoth* to save the colony."

"But that means you'd have to…" Morales watched as Benedict nodded. "You can't be serious. That would be mutiny. Treason."

"I believe Hans is deadly serious," Zhang said.

"It would be mutiny, but treason? To whom? The Sway government betrayed the human race. I had family on Earth. We all did and those power-crazed bureaucrats killed them all but managed to save themselves. *They* are the traitors. Every soldier of the Host took an oath to serve with honor and protect lives. What's honorable about leaving half a million people to die to save people who committed genocide? Some wise men once wrote that in the course of human events it becomes necessary for people to dissolve the political bounds which have connected them and it has never applied more than to those two hundred. If we go to get them, it should be to arrest them as war criminals and have them stand trial. Not to rescue them so they can go rule over the largest colony world they can reach."

"What about the crew?" Morales said.

"We invoke the moral right of an officer to relieve their commander if they are unfit for duty," Benedict said.

"It has been my experience that soldiers will follow the commanding officers which means command would have to be assumed quickly and decisively," Zhang said. "And within the next ten hours or we will be too late to stop the asteroids."

"Even if they do back us, the crew is not enough. Dailey has the thimble," Morales said. There were only five thimbles made and given to the highest-ranking members of the Host. Each was a controller that fit over the wearer's thumb like its namesake but allowed the wearer complete control over all ships, sky stations, weapons, and equipment of the Host. It allowed its wearer to take direct control of any asset in the entire military. That included firearms. The only limitation was they had to be in proximity to assert that authority. The exception would be if the commanding officer of a ship was willing to cede authority via the communication system. "If we killed Dailey, he wouldn't be able to countermand what we're doing, but we would lose control of crucial systems of the ship and any moral authority we might be claiming. And if he used the thimble to lock in the course, we wouldn't be able to turn around until we reached Earth and the settlers would already be dead. It's pointless."

"Maybe not entirely pointless," Zhang said.

"Just incredibly difficult. The Host had several sappers come up with scenarios on how they would try to override or steal a thimble. They then built fail-safes into the system based on what we came up with," Benedict said. "However, since Dailey forced himself into command here, I have run new scenarios in my mind."

"My former commanding officer was also asked to be part of the same project and had many of us junior officers do the same. I too have come up with other options in the interim. It would be prudent for us to pool our knowledge to figure out the best way to take command of the ship," Zhang said.

"If we lead an outright rebellion, some will follow orders, others their oath to protect life. Soldier would fight against soldier. It would cause a schism in our crew that might never be healed," Benedict said. "Not to mention the loss of life. That is unacceptable and something I will not be a part of. We need to do something else."

"There's something else we need to consider if we relieve Daily of his command," Zhang said. "There is no longer a Sway government. *Behemoth* will be one of the last flagships left intact. Perhaps the only one. We would be assuming command indefinitely. We would, by default, become the ultimate authority on this ship and possibly over any other ships that survive. This is not something to be entered into lightly."

"Yes, because we're already taking rebellion and mutiny far too casually," Morales said.

"We've got less than ten hours to make this happen, so let's get to work. We'll start with who else we can trust," Benedict said.

In too short a time, they returned to the General's ready room.

"All right people, we have less than four days in transit to enact a rescue plan, so let me hear your best ideas," General Dailey said.

Captain Shannon Morales stood up. "I'm sorry, sir, but there's no plan that makes any sense." She trained her sidearm on the General as ten armed men and women took the room. Colonel Zhang had a gun in each hand and was covering the rest of the table. "You have proven yourself unfit for command and we are relieving you of duty."

"You are a traitor! All of you are. This is mutiny and treason and I will see you all executed for this." The General pressed on his metal-covered thumb then brought it up to his mouth and said, "Lockdown!"

Normally, the soldiers' guns would have been locked and weapons would have dropped from the ceiling, targeted everyone in the room not wearing the thimble, and shot them dead. Nothing happened.

"Nice try, General but we already accommodated for your thimble. It's quite useless in here. Now if you will kindly give the order to return to Diamondhead to save the colonists this will go well. Should you choose to do otherwise we may be forced to resort to violence," Zhang said.

"You think you can intimidate me?! You're a fool, Colonel. It's only a matter of time before ship security takes this room and ends the lot of you," Dailey said.

Zhang smiled. "I guess we better finish this quickly then."

The colonel's right hand twisted and he fired at the General but in the instant before the bullet struck, Major Benedict leaped in front of the General. Benedict fell to the floor holding his gut as dark crimson liquid spilled out.

"You chose the wrong side, Benedict. I'm sorry you don't have the stomach for what needs to be done. This is the only way," Zhang said. "Clear the room. I'll assume command of the ship while these two stay here to think about the error of their ways."

The rebel soldiers led the rest of the ranking officers out of the room but two of them stayed on guard duty outside of the door.

"Hans, are you okay?" Dailey said.

"It's a bad gut wound, so not so much, sir," Benedict grunted.

"Benedict, I know I treated you poorly and sent you on more than your share of dangerous missions but you certainly proved your mettle here today," Dailey said.

"Just doing my duty as a soldier."

"To be honest, if I had to pick the officer most likely to shoot me before today, I would've chosen you, especially since I know you disagree with my decision," Dailey said.

"I do. I think you made a huge mistake allowing those people to die, but if there is one thing I've learned in more than twenty years as a sapper it's that violence is never the best answer." Benedict took off his uniform shirt and folded it up and placed it over the wound that soaked through his t-shirt. "Why didn't your thimble work?"

"I don't know. They're supposed to be impossible to

jam."

"They must have removed the shut-off circuits in their guns. Maybe they managed to set up some sort of jamming device in combination with overwhelming all input channels in the area. It could block you from connecting with the ship by making sure there was no connection available. It's what I would've tried. But its range would be limited. They wouldn't be able to do it throughout the entire ship."

The general stroked his chin. "How long would they be able to make something like that last?"

"If it's tied into the ship's power, indefinitely. If we can get you to a different part of the ship, the thimble should work. We need a way to get you out of here," Benedict said.

Dailey shook his head. "Morales is a little softhearted but there's no way Zhang would allow me out of the jammed zone for any reason."

Benedict grimaced and held the shirt tighter to his stomach which gave Daily an idea.

"They'd never let me but you need medical attention. I could give you control of the thimble and then as soon as you're clear, you could stop them and send ship security to get me out of here."

"It's a lovely thought but let's lay our cards on the table. Why would you think I'd give it back to you?" Benedict said.

Dailey grinned. "Simple really. I'm a five-star general. You're a major. The soldiers aboard the ship will listen to whatever I say. A previous owner of the thimble can still use it. If you don't give it back to me, I will simply have your hand cut off or maybe just have you shot. As soon as I put the thimble on, it will respond to my commands again. Do this and I will make you a Colonel, stop the ship, and allow you to head back to Diamondhead with the resources you need to destroy to divert or destroy those asteroids. Do we have a deal?"

"So, you give me control of the thimble, I get you out of this room, and I'm allowed to save the people of Diamondhead and then you will use force to take back the thimble if needed," Benedict said.

"Yes."

"We have a deal," Benedict said.

The General pressed the top of the thimble and said, "Transfer protocol Omega."

The General grimaced as if he was suddenly in pain and he undid the thimble strap. His thumb tip was bleeding, the thimble's final validation of his DNA ensuring the transfer wasn't done by voice command alone.

Dailey handed Benedict the thimble. "Put it on your left thumb, press the top and say 'Transfer protocol Alpha.' It'll take a sample of your DNA and you'll be able to control the thimble and the ship long enough to get me out of here."

Benedict fastened the strap around his hand and wrist then pressed the button and said, "Transfer protocol Alpha." Benedict didn't even flinch as a needle stuck his thumb and took a sample of his DNA.

General Dailey smirked then got up and banged on the door. "This man needs a surgeon, goddammit. He's a soldier of the Host and deserves medical care, whatever you think of me."

The door opened and Captain Shannon Morales came in with two medics and a stretcher gurney. Her gun never pointed anywhere but at the general. "We're not savages. We were already on our way."

The man and the woman medics gently lifted Benedict onto the stretcher and rushed him out of the room.

As soon as the door closed, Shanna Morales asked, "Did it work?"

Benedict gave her a thumbs up and sat up on the edge of the gurney. He pulled off his t-shirt and the simulated wound pack that was a part of every sapper's bag of tricks in case they needed to fake injury or death on a mission.

"How long until the ship systems reboot is done?" Benedict said.

"Finished two minutes ago so if he had tried his thimble again before giving it to you, it would've worked. Making the systems unavailable was the only way to make sure the thimble couldn't connect. Did he buy your jamming scenario?"

"Obviously. You have a cell prepared for him?"

Morales nodded.

"Take the General to the cell and have him guarded around the clock by soldiers you know we can trust. If he gets hold of the thimble, he can take control back," Benedict said. "Now let's get this ship turned around. Five hours to spare is not a window I'm comfortable with."


It took more than four days before Major Hans Benedict went to visit Dailey in the brig. Unsurprisingly, the General was not exactly pleased to see him.

"Hello, General."

"How are you enjoying the fruits of your treasonous labors?" Dailey said.

"We destroyed the small asteroid and diverted the larger two into an orbit that will eventually take them into the sun. They will not bother the people of Diamondhead again. I accomplished what I set out to."

Dailey smirked. "I guess then you will be returning the thimble and control of *Behemoth* to me now that you've completed your mission."

"No sir, I don't think that would be a good idea," Benedict said.

"Even if it breaks our deal? I guess that just proves what a lying, treasonous bastard you really are."

"I kept my end of the bargain. I made sure you got out of the ready room. Our bargain never mentioned where you would end up. I took the resources I needed to stop the asteroids. You are out of shape, General, but you are welcome to try and take the thimble back from me by force as we agreed."

"It seems you made that a little bit more difficult by not bringing it with you."

"The thimble is a powerful tool but it could also be a crutch. I am not going to lead by threats and intimidation but by example and honor."

Dailey snorted. "With honor? You know nothing of the meaning of the word. I suppose you'll be wanting me to address you as general now."

"Not in the least. This was not a coup but the relieving of an officer with impaired judgment from command for the greater good. I'll stick with my current rank."

"Greater good, my ass. I suppose you're going to entirely ignore rescuing your superiors."

"As a matter of fact, I am." Benedict pulled out a small communication screen.

Right after the reboot, Major Benedict was logged in as the commanding officer by way of the thimble but it's possible the General had a way to override that and it was best not to take any chances. All contact with the main ship had been stripped from Dailey's cell and the surrounding areas to ensure that the General could not get back into the system.

"I know you would never believe me if I told you that I had proof that we were right and you were wrong. Instead, I'm going to show it to you. We made contact this morning with the *Gargantuan* which had returned to Earth."

Benedict started the recording and an ash-covered face in a ragged uniform appeared on the screen.

"*Behemoth*, this is Sergeant Warhol. As the highest-ranking soldier still alive on board the *Gargantuan*, I am the commanding officer. After clearing the surrounding area and having our dropships destroyed, we managed to land *Gargantuan* in order to rescue the heads of the Sway. Almost immediately our ship was boarded by the creature's foot soldiers."

The sergeant transmitted images of small and large creatures that had appendages that undulated like tentacles but had razor-sharp cilia and maws along the appendages slithering along the hull. The recording showed them boarding *Gargantuan* and killing thousands of soldiers. The final recorded images Warhol transmitted showed thousands of the nightmare creatures in the corridors of the ship, all heading toward the bridge from where the sergeant was transmitting.

"The creatures appear to have changed their tactics. We thought we had outsmarted them when we managed to land but in fact, that was just what they wanted us to do. They must have realized that humanity had spread to the stars so they have taken over the *Gargantuan* with plans to go after the colony worlds and wipe out what survives of humanity. We left a beacon in orbit beyond the moon. I uploaded a warning to make sure no ship ever goes near the planet, but I need you to destroy *Gargantuan* before they take the bridge. Despite being in command, I do not have sufficient rank to activate *Gargantuan's* self-destruct but I know your General has a thimble. I will slave our ship's controls to it so he can prevent these creatures from leaving Earth." The banging on the blast doors got louder. "And it needs to be done now."

Everyone on the bridge of the *Behemoth,* including Zhang and Morales, looked to Benedict.

"Sergeant Warhol, General Dailey has turned control of his thimble over to me. Slave the controls of the *Gargantuan* on my mark and I will activate the self-destruct. Mark."

The view switched as Warhol set the controls as the blast door started to crack from the pounding from without. "It's done, Major. Hurry."

Benedict spoke into the thimble and again didn't flinch when the needle sampled his blood. "Self-destruct is set for ten seconds. You're a good man Sergeant Warhol and you've just saved untold millions of lives. I regret that we cannot return the favor and save yours."

The view switched again as Major Benedict and the rest of the bridge crew brought their hands to their foreheads in a salute.

"I'm only doing my duty as a soldier but thank you, sir." Sergeant Warhol snapped to attention and returned the salute and held it as creatures of nightmare tore through the door and launched themselves through the air like a swarm of screaming chainsaws toward him. Before they could reach the brave man, *Gargantuan's* self-destruct blew them all to ash and dust.

Major Benedict turned off the screen.

"So, you see if we had followed those orders and your plan, the people of Diamondhead would be wiped out, our crew would be dead, and those creatures would've had not one but two Colossus-class warships to use to wipe out humanity from its new home among the stars. I only hope that now you can see that you were in the wrong and that we did the only thing we could."

"You think that excuses mutiny? Think again. I could have used the thimble to destroy that ship and we could have utilized this intel to come up with a new plan and still saved those people."

"General, we would have gotten there first. *Gargantuan* wouldn't have had a thimble to return the favor. That could have been us."

"We would have never let that happen. You disobeyed a direct order and committed treason against a general of the Host. I will get out of this cell and I will see that all you traitors are executed for what you've done."

"Sir, I always felt you were a fool, an idiot, and a vain, egotistical little man but I never actually thought you were evil until now."

"Then why don't you kill me so I don't make good on my threats?" Dailey said.

"Because we're better soldiers than you."

"You don't understand the meaning of the word. A soldier is better because he is stronger and more ruthless than those he is fighting. Your idea of better is going to get you and everyone else under your traitorous command killed," Dailey said.

"Or maybe it will wind up making the universe a better place. Good day, General."

Benedict left the cell. Colonel Zhang and Captain

Morales were waiting outside.

"How did it go?" Morales said.

"Not well. Daily can't entertain the possibility that he might've been wrong," Benedict said.

"You were expecting something different?" Zhang said.

"No, but I may have had the tiniest bit of hope. We'll have to let the crew know that from here on out, rank is going to be a meritocracy. In light of that, Captain Morales, I hereby appoint you as my second-in-command."

"But Hans, I'm only a captain. There are many more experienced and high-ranking officers than me including Colonel Zhang," Morales said.

Zhang shook his head. "I enjoy finding out things and putting what I've learned together in order to see how situations are going to play out. I don't want to waste my time being in charge of an entire ship. I'm perfectly okay with my current position."

"And as for all those other more experienced and high-ranking officers, when it came down to saving half a million people, they were all willing to keep their mouths shut rather than doing the right thing. That is not how things are going to work anymore. You risked your career and possible execution to do the right thing. You've earned this position. I think once the crew sees how things now work that we will be very impressed by what they accomplish."

"What are we going to do now?" Captain Morales said.

"There are a lot of people out there on a lot of different worlds. We are the last surviving Colossus-class ship. What are we going to do? We are going do our duty."

# DIVINING EVEREST

"**I** do not recognize your authority."

The sound that escaped Major Hans Benedict was somewhere between a chuckle and a sigh. "Not the first time I've heard that. In fact, I get that a lot. That still doesn't change the fact that I have a Colossus-class warship in orbit around this planet with enough fire power to reduce you to ash."

The vampire on the throne shook his head from side to side. It was his turn to laugh. "I would think that someone of your rank in the Host would know a bit more about vampire physiology. Light is not going to reduce us to ash."

"But particle weapons would do a pretty good job of it. Although if you are so comfortable with sunlight why don't we adjourn to your courtyard in some swim trunks? I'm more than willing to catch some rays if you are," said Benedict.

"I think not." The vampire closed his hands beneath his chin and rested his head atop them. He knew very well that while sunlight would not kill a vampire, an hour in it without protection would make him too ill to do much of anything for the better part of a week. "In fact, I don't even think you remember me."

"I'll take that bet. What are you willing to wager?"

"Against you, nothing of importance. Even as a private, you had a reputation."

"Nice try, but we never met until I was a lieutenant. And you, Longstrum, were nothing but a lowly, blood-sucking grunt in the 101ˢᵗ Starborne Vampire Brigade."

"I'm impressed. It's been more than fifteen years. And it doesn't look like many of them have been kind to you. Can I offer you a taste of immortality?" mocked the vampire, knowing full well that he would never even try to turn the major.

Benedict suppressed the shiver of revulsion at the thought. "Surely, you do not believe the hype yourself. The longest vampire in service to the Sway clocked out at about 125 years."

"But he was a soldier and, if I remember correctly, died fighting a human battle."

"That's what soldiers do. And as far as I am aware you were never given any discharge papers."

"So you've come all this way to recruit me back in the fold as a soldier?"

"Hardly," Benedict spat. His disdain for the Sway's monster troops was widely known. "I'm here in answer to a distress signal."

"I certainly didn't send a distress signal and I am the rightful and duly elected governor of this planet."

"Really? It was my understanding that Everest had a population of almost 600,000 humans and less than a thousand bloodsuckers. Unless you've managed to breed." The virus that caused vampirism had been around on Earth for hundreds of years. Despite popular lore, a simple bite of a vampire or even drinking a vampire's blood was not enough to turn someone. In fact, only rarely would someone react well enough to the virus in order to become an actual vampire. Otherwise, they would have long ago overrun the Earth. The Sway scientists managed to genetically alter the virus in two very crucial ways. They made it much easier for it to take effect in soldiers. This was done by infecting them with a retro virus beforehand, which left the cells more susceptible to the change. It also had the interesting secondary effect of stopping the virus from being able to spread beyond the initial host.

Longstrum smiled. "I'd hardly tell you if we had."

"Technically, you still hold the rank of sergeant. I am a superior officer. If I order you to tell me, you will tell me."

"I am no longer a soldier. I never wanted to be in the first place. Tell me Benedict—you enlisted, correct?" The major nodded. "I did not. I wasn't even drafted. I was chosen because mandatory genetic tests indicated that I would be a likely candidate for successful turning. I was taken from my home in the middle of the night, strapped to a table, and turned into what I am today, screaming all the way. I had a wife and three children. I never saw them again. They are still back on Earth. Or they were."

"We all lost family in the conflagration."

"Yes, however your *Behemoth* is rumored to be the only Colossus that did not return to Earth in its hour of greatest need."

"Which is why we are the only remaining Colossus-class warship."

"That means you disobeyed direct orders. In fact, the story is you staged a coup d'état, taking over your ship and deposing General Daily. Or perhaps you have assumed that rank."

Benedict narrowed his brows and his pupils became much smaller. "I am still a major." Benedict had not assumed a greater rank precisely because he did not want it to seem like a coup. He felt the orders were detrimental and believed in an officer's duty to do the right thing, sometimes despite orders.

"I will not follow an order from a traitor. That in itself would be treason, if I still cared enough to be a soldier."

Benedict ignored the dig. "I received a call from humans who claimed to have been enslaved by you. I am here to negotiate their freedom, by any means necessary."

"That is utter nonsense. We have no slaves. The humans of Everest are free to live their lives as they would, except on occasion they must feed us."

"That doesn't sound awful free to me."

"Even you know nothing is free. We protect them. We have ended hunger and poverty. We do not allow any of the humans to be killed or even harmed. Their blood is collected in a hospital setting where great care is taken, even to minimize scaring. With the size of the population and an average human life span of seventy-five years, it is unlikely that any human would have to be used for feeding more than once every three or four years. Hardly unreasonable."

"You claim to be the elected governor. But were any humans allowed to vote in this so-called election?"

"Of course not. We could hardly trust their decisions, now could we? When humans were in charge look at what happened to Earth. There is no war on Everest. There are not even any soldiers, yourself and your honor guard excluded."

"Which I find interesting since I understand when this system's Colossus returned to Earth they left a contingent of soldiers to watch over this planet."

"They left a hundred men and 917 vampires. Not good odds. Why would anyone in the Host even think we would take orders for long? Especially once they ran out of the drugs that they laced our blood with." Benedict raised an eyebrow. "You didn't know? Apparently, much of our craving for blood was not natural. We were fed drugs. When the effects wore off, we mistook the cravings as hunger for blood. Made us incredibly effective and deadly on the battlefield as they withheld our meals beforehand. But they only left behind so much drugged blood and the soldiers soon… left their assignments. The withdrawal was… unpleasant to say the least. But once the drugs were out of our systems, we were able to think clearly. It did not take much for us to facilitate the shift of power within our ranks. There were a few regrettable deaths but the majority of those men and women were allowed to resign their commissions and take up lives as citizens."

"I see. I'm going to have to ask you to hold free elections and turn over control of the government to whoever is elected by the entire planet. You were soldiers. You have earned your rights. You should all have a vote, but so should everyone on this planet."

"That's very magnanimous of you, Benedict. A definite change of policy from the Sway government which would never allow any of their monster troops any rights, other than the chance to be soldiers for the rest of their existence. Otherwise, why would we give up what we already have for a guarantee of losing it?"

"Because I told you to."

"Now Benedict, you have twelve soldiers with you. I have more vampires than that in this room. Do you think even the thirteen of you could defeat us before we ended you?"

Benedict smiled. "I fought with and against monsters. I give us better than even odds. Of course, that won't stop my people from leveling this city."

"The city is shared by vampires and humans alike.

We both know many more humans would die from your friendly fire than vampires and that really would ruin the purpose of what you claim you are trying to do."

"True, but there is the option of a more surgical strike."

"Your 142nd Starborne may have the upper hand in fire power, but surgical strikes would require Harpy dropships to invade our air space and we have enough planetary defenses to shoot them out of the sky. We allowed yours to land as a courtesy."

"And don't think we don't appreciate that. Of course, I and a few of my people had already been on Everest for the better part of a week when the Harpy landed." The vampire's eyebrows rose at Benedict's words. "I assume you remember what my specialty is?"

"You are a sapper." The term was taken from a French military position from the 1700s, the modern sapper specialized in infiltrating enemy ships and territory for the purpose of sabotage or destruction. Benedict was legendary.

"You're bluffing."

"Maybe, but you really want to call me on it?"

"Absolutely. There is no way you landed without us picking you up on sensors. The *Behemoth* has been in orbit for less than a day. There is no possibility you are not bluffing. You will not intimidate us simply because there are a few exaggerated stories of your skills."

Benedict's head tilted to the side and he shrugged his shoulders. "So be it." He pressed a button on a metal cylinder that was hidden in the palm of his hand and threw it to the vampire. "I suggest you evacuate 927 High Street."

"The blood depository?"

"I figured the best way to your hearts was through your stomachs. That or with small arms fire. I'd hurry, Longstrum.

You only have thirty minutes."

The vampire leader shouted for the building to be evacuated. It took exactly eighteen minutes until every soul was out of the building. After exactly thirty minutes explosives knocked out support beams from the basement to the upper floor, imploding it into a pile of rubble. Neither the building to its left nor its right was harmed.

"Arrest Benedict and his soldiers," Longstrum ordered.

The soldiers of the 142$^{nd}$ lifted their weapons higher. Benedict held up a hand. "Very well. But you only have twelve hours until the next building. And twelve hours until the building after that. We planted enough to go for two weeks. Any harm comes to me or my people and I won't tell you where the next one is in time for you to evacuate."

"And you call me the monster? Away with them."

Benedict nodded for his men to allow the vampires to disarm them. A suicidal battle served no benefit. The soldiers were shackled and brought down to the basement of the planetary capital building.

"I suppose you have to throw us in and find some room among all your other human prisoners," Benedict said.

Longstrum looked at the major as if he were insane. "We have no human prisoners in this city at this time."

Benedict didn't believe him, but when they were taken into the jail, the cells were mostly empty. The members of the 142$^{nd}$ Starborne were put four to a cell, with Benedict getting his own. There was only one other prisoner, a woman vampire. The soldiers closed the metal doors and left them with two vampire guards.

"Ah, company at last," said the female vampire.

"Rose, shut up," said one of the two guards.

The lady vampire gave them the finger and continued

to speak. "You look like you are playing soldier, but humans aren't allowed to be soldiers anymore. What did you do to get in here?"

"Objected to humans being kept as slaves."

"Who is keeping slaves? Will they be joining us too?"

Benedict furrowed his brow. "What are you in for?"

The vampire Rose made a spitting sound. "I killed a human and they put me in here for that, if you can believe it. I understand why they don't want us to kill them as a whole—it makes for too much unrest, but there are so many of them. What difference does one more or less make?"

"I supposed you would have to ask his family that," said Benedict.

"Oh pish. Only more blood bags. What bothers them is really unimportant. But for killing one of them I get twenty-five years in a cell, being forced to suck blood out of a plastic bag. What kind of life is that? They should have just killed me."

Benedict actually agreed but held his tongue. "Why didn't they?"

"Because Cyrus Longstrum outlawed capital punishment. For vampires I can understand, but to include humans? So for one little indiscretion I've got to spend my life in here? It isn't right."

"Sir," whispered Colonel Leon Juma, a fellow sapper who had made planetfall with Benedict. "Are you going to call in an assault team and get us out of here?"

Benedict had lain down on his bunk and put his feet up, his hands laced behind his head. "I don't think it will be necessary. I have a feeling we won't be in here too long."

It was less than twelve hours before his words proved prophetic. The door to the cells exploded inward, knocking the vampire guards to the ground. The blast was followed by a handful of humans carrying assault rifles.

"You've only got moments before the bloodsuckers manage to mount a defense. Get those sky boys out," ordered the man who appeared to be in charge.

Benedict didn't bother to correct the fact that three of his assault team were female. He was actually surprised two of his sapper team, Corporal Shila Bangi and Captain Ami Chang, hadn't done it themselves. He surmised that they, like himself, found it bad manners to correct someone who was rescuing them, and listening and observing was an effective way of gathering information.

The man in charge stood in front of Benedict's cell at attention and saluted. Benedict raised an eyebrow, then stood to return the salute.

"You are the voice of freedom?" Benedict said, using the sign-off the distress call had ended with.

"Yes sir, Major Benedict sir." The man leaning in and whispered, "I was Private First Class Adrian Voice when the bloodsuckers overwhelmed us, sir. We didn't want to concede control but our fighting them would have ended in too many deaths so we pretended to go back to civilian life but instead went underground. We put up a good fight, sir."

Benedict nodded. "How many are you?"

"Of the original soldiers, there are fifteen including me, sir. However, we have over one hundred freedom fighters actively engaging the enemy in this city alone. Stand back sir, we are going to get you out of there."

Several men in the rescue party had placed small amounts of plastic explosives over the cell locks. Members of the 142nd Starborne stepped to the back of their cells, using their mattresses for additional cover. Former Private

First Class Voice hit a button on a device on his belt and all the locks were shattered with the small explosions.

"Nice work, soldier."

"Thank you, sir."

"How about getting me out?" said the vampire prisoner.

Voice got a crap-eating grin on his face and pulled his sidearm pointing it between the eyes of the vampire. "I'll be happy to set you free. The ultimate freedom." The vampire stepped back from the bars, nervously looking around for a place to hide from a bullet. The cell didn't provide any cover and her speed and strength didn't mean much in such a small space. Voice cocked back the hammer on his sidearm. Benedict's hand fell across the gun, his finger landing between the hammer and the barrel.

"Host soldiers do not kill in cold blood, son." Voice's eyes darted to the pair of vampire guards the initial blast had knocked out. "That includes the unconscious." He turned to the vampire prisoner. "Tell Longstrom because we were freed, even though not by him, I will deactivate the explosives." He turned back to Voice. "Let's go. I assume you have an escape route mapped out."

"Of course, sir. Please follow me."

In the age of satellite tracking and video surveillance, breaking into a prison and getting out without having an escape route noticed was extremely challenging. The human freedom fighters were up to the task. They had managed a small power outage which disabled most of the local surveillance and waited for the skies to be overcast in order to provide cloud cover from the eyes in the sky.

Vampires did have enhanced hearing, sight, and smell, but they weren't exactly bloodhounds. However just to be on the safe side the area was doused with a methane compound designed to eliminate any hope of olfactory tracking.

The human's hideout at first glance wasn't much of a hideout at all. It was a bowling alley. The Earth sport had remained popular on many of the settled worlds and most large towns had at least one bowling alley. This one was owned by former Private First Class Voice. His logic was sound when he explained that humans hiding and sneaking in, knocking on doors and using passwords were all too suspicious to cope with modern surveillance techniques. However, all he had to do was make sure his teams were groups of four and they were easy enough to pass off as a group just interested in a chance at knocking down three hundred pins. And groups of people coming in and out, especially on league night, would hardly raise an eyebrow on an interested bloodsucker. Of course. thirteen men and women in Sway black uniforms with 142$^{nd}$ Starborne patches on the sleeves more than likely would. The first thing that they did before going to the bowling alley was to change into civilian clothing.

'Ihey reached the alley without incident.

"Benedict, pick three of your people and go to lane seven, me and my people will take lane eight. That way we can talk," Voice said.

Private Ricco Jonas, the last member of the sapper team, stepped up to the major's ear. "Sir, this operation is totally amateur, we need to post guards. To bowl when work needs to be done …"

"Any posted guards would attract attention. We have video surveillance covering three hundred and sixty degrees of the building including the rooftops and surrounding streets. If somebody should come in all they will see are people out on the town bowling and drinking. There will be nobody milling about whispering to raise suspicions," Voice countered.

Benedict raised an eyebrow and nodded slowly. "It's not how we would do things, Jonas, but it seems to have worked so far for them. For the moment we will follow Mr. Voice's lead. However, there is no reason why a couple of people at the bar couldn't be staring into their glasses which just happen to be in view of each of the doorways."

"Yes, sir. I'll take care of it."

"I also see that Voice has karaoke. Perhaps you can help block any listening devices and enjoy yourself at the same time." Benedict and the rest of the sappers were all too aware of Rico's love of opera and his proficiency in singing both loud and well.

Private Jonas smiled. "I think I might be able to manage that, although I doubt I will need a microphone."

"Not in a place this size. Try not to knock out any of the glass. And I think I speak on behalf of all the sappers, anything but Donizetti's *The Daughter of the Regiment*."

"Spoilsport. Just for that, I'm going to go all Gilbert and Sullivan on your ass."

Benedict rolled his eyes, chose his team, and picked out a bowling ball.

The major allowed Voice to go first and observed how he threw. He knocked seven of the ten pins. Voice picked up the spare. Benedict stepped up to the line aimed and threw. The major got a strike.

"Impressive, Major. When is the last time you went bowling?" asked Voice.

"At least twenty years ago. Was back in my academy days."

"That makes that especially remarkable, but from all I have heard about you it doesn't surprise me. I have to tell you we were all impressed when we heard what you did."

Benedict ignored the comment, which he usually did when someone brought up his mutiny. As a lifelong officer and soldier, he did not regard what he had done as something to be admired. However, the idea of sending the entire ship and its crew to certain death and abandoning the people they were protecting to certain doom was even more so.

"Please explain to me exactly what help you expect from us or what help you would like from us in your fight here," Benedict said as the next bowler stepped up.

"We have the numbers in theory, but too many of the people are willing to let the status quo lie. They don't want to rock the boat. They still get to go to work and come home to their families. They don't seem to care that one or more bloodsuckers are ignoring Longstrom's rules and actively killing humans around the city. We covertly patrol to find the vamp or vamps who have been killing humans in the streets. The fact that anyone of them can become a cocktail to a bloodsucker at any time by random killing or government order doesn't seem to faze most of them. However, there are those of us that find the idea of bloodsuckers ruling humans too repulsive to let slide. We plan to get rid of their power by any means necessary."

"I see. And assuming you're able to do that, what is your plan for the government afterward?"

Voice narrowed his brow. "We would set up an intern government until we could return to planetary elections. The officers in the freedom fighters would take over government tasks for that time period."

"With you of course at the helm?"

Misunderstanding the tone of the question, Voice grinned widely. "Of course. Have to have someone in charge who can be trusted to make the right choices. And the hard ones."

"How do you think you can do this? What are your estimates in terms of collateral losses?" In the company of his own officers and people, Benedict avoided terms like collateral losses. It was just fancy words for people having to die to obtain the objective but he knew all too well when to cloak horrible deeds in shiny words.

"Of course, we want to minimize any civilian casualties. However, there are those who are working with the bloodsuckers and those who have chosen to betray their own kind. We are not quite so concerned about them. We have given thoughts to poison and have even tried it. However, the bloodsuckers are too well organized. They don't simply just pick a person at random to feed off of. They choose, then put them in isolation for a week, making sure that they are the only ones providing food and drink. That way they can be sure that the blood they devour is not tainted. We lost three good people during the isolation period."

"You poisoned your own people?"

"Their numbers came up in the lottery and they volunteered. It wasn't something we wanted to do. It is not something that I'm proud of, but I am proud of those three men who gave their lives in hopes of ending the vampire occupation."

Benedict grew silent and it was his turn to bowl again. It was obvious his mind was elsewhere because this time he didn't make the strike, instead leaving up the seven and ten pins.

"Tough break. That's the hardest spare there is."

"There is a huge difference between hard and impossible," Benedict said. Moving a step to his right he put his thumb up lining it up with one pin and then the other as if it were a sight on a rifle. He drew back his arm and let the ball fly. It rolled down the edge of the alley hitting the ten pin at just the right angle to send it spinning leftward to knock down the seven pin.

"Amazing."

Benedict ignored the comment and moved to the side to allow the next bowler to use the lane.

"Tell me more about what you have tried so far."

"We have managed to get two of them with snipers. Another was alone on the street and we managed to overpower him and separate his head from his neck."

Despite the myths, stake and decapitation were not the only ways to kill a vampire. Enough damage to the body would do the trick. However, fresh human blood was almost a miracle drug, inducing cellular regeneration more than one hundred times faster than would normally be possible in a human. As long as the heart was not blocked from healing and the head not removed from the body, a vampire could theoretically heal from almost any wound with enough blood. Of course, fire destroyed the cells beyond their ability to regenerate.

"Have you tried protests or civil disobedience?" Benedict asked.

"Hell, no. We weren't dumb enough to fall into those traps, sir. That would simply alert them to who we were and assure that we were watched at all times."

"Have they done any harm to any of the citizens of

Everest?"

"You mean besides drinking their blood and telling them what they can and can't do? No, there have been no public executions. In fact, they have puppet human judges to preside over trials. Even human cops. They have most people fooled, but not us."

"I'm going to need a few days to get the lay of the land." Benedict didn't bother to explain that the time he spent before meeting with the vampire ruler was primarily concerned with getting to know his way around and finding both soft and hard targets to plant explosives on. Most of that time was spent trying to avoid casualties. He did not have much time to interact with the general populous.

"I'd be happy to take you around and introduce you to some people," said Voice.

Benedict shook his head. "I will do better alone."

"But your face is on all the video feeds. They will spot you and you will be arrested."

"If they catch me, I deserve to be caught." Benedict changed his posture, seeming to shrink two inches and become a meek overweight man instead of the older but well-muscled soldier that he was. His facial muscles relaxed giving him a different appearance. As soon as time permitted, he would die his hair.

Many people compared sappers to the legend of ninjas who were able to blend into the shadows and disappear at will. Benedict considered ninjas a thing of legend, but they did have some things in common. Neither dressed up in funny costumes for one. Sappers did their best to blend in, to not draw attention to themselves. It was why he liked Voice's idea of having his meetings in the bowling alley, simply because it would not arouse much suspicion.

Benedict was not so thrilled with some other things he saw and needed to sort them out for himself.

At the scheduled time, Hans Benedict returned to the bowling alley and had a round in the bar room with his men.

"So what's the plan, sir?" asked Captain Leon Juma.

"These freedom fighters are fighting against something that's not really there. I don't like the idea of a group of bloodsuckers ruling over humans any more than anyone else does, but as far as governments go, they are quite benevolent. There's no record of any lottery "winner" being harmed. The vampires who hunt and kill on their own are punished. The bloodsuckers are protecting the humans. Humans who commit crimes are not coddled but not tortured either. The punishments seem sufficient to actually deter crime."

"Are they protecting them because it is the right thing to do or because they do not want to lose their food source?" asked Juma.

Benedict shrugged. "In the long run, what difference does it make? The people here are a lot better off than on a lot of the other worlds we have seen. We are not going to get involved in this fight."

"Are we going to turn over Voice and his people?"

"I don't like the idea. I don't think they have much chance in succeeding in anything other than being a thorn in the vampires' collective asses. Voice was right about somebody killing humans, but disturbingly, those responsible are making it look like the bloodsuckers are doing it. There are at least six victims."

"What makes you think the vamps aren't?" asked Juma.

"The wounds were wrong. Two very nice, neat bite marks on the two victims I managed to sneak in and examine."

Juma frowned. "Any vamp wounds I've ever seen have had chunks torn out, usually chewed over pretty good."

"Exactly, although the vamps may feed differently when off the Sway's drugged feed," Benedict said.

"So Longstrum's covering it up?"

"The opposite. He's offering a reward for information leading to the arrest of the killer."

"You think Voice is behind it?"

"It has crossed my mind."

"So what's the plan?"

"I want to speak with Voice. If he is the killer… well, I hope he's not. "

"How will you know for sure?"

"I won't, but if it's not him I think we should call *Behemoth* for evac and let Everest sort this out itself."

Benedict went back up to the bartender. "Where is Voice?"

The man serving drinks smiled. "We are so happy to have you with us, Major Benedict. Mr. Voice left this envelope for you. He knew you would be back today and he was very excited to show you that he really meant business."

Benedict took the envelope and tore the end open pulling out the paper inside. "God damn it."

"What is it, sir?"

"Voice got it in his head that this is the time to do or die. Unfortunately, a lot more people are going to be in the die column than the do. All right, we are not leaving yet. Everybody suit up. Juma, comm *Behemoth*. I want Harpies moving planetside now. We have a massacre to stop."

The baker's dozen of the 142nd Starborne double-timed it through the streets in full uniforms and battle gear. Benedict used his headset to break into the civilian communications net.

"To all civilian authorities, this is Major Hans Benedict of the 142nd Starborne. A group of terrorists are planning to blow up the civil hall building. Immediately evacuate it. We have several Harpies with my people on the way. We will help with evacuations and disarming any explosives. Do not fire on them."

"Benedict," said a familiar voice over the radio. "What are you trying to pull? Blowing up another building?"

"Longstrum, I don't like the fact that your kind is in charge of this planet, but my recon has led me to believe that you are, if not a benevolent force, at least one that is not doing harm. There are a group of humans who have decided to kill those humans whom they believe are conspiring with vampires, which means any civil servant. I speculate that they may even be the ones responsible for your recent murders. I am not going to allow innocent civilians to be killed. Therefore my people and I are at your disposal. In fact, since we have more experience with this kind of thing, I respectfully suggest that we take command of the mission."

"I don't trust you, Benedict…"

"Cyrus, you are going to have to. You don't need to be dealing with this and a firefight with my men. Just evacuate the damn building and meet me on site. Benedict out."

Benedict and his dozen Host soldiers reached the government building where chaos was having its way with all in its path. Civilians were crowding the streets and four Harpies were hovering in the air over the building. Four hundred members of the 142$^{nd}$ Starborne were moving onto the ground, attempting crowd control by herding the people as far away from the building as possible.

A captain at a mobile command post signed Benedict to join her. "We've made contact, Major Benedict. They have taken the entire daycare center hostage. They're saying if the humans do not rise up and kill the vampires, all the children will die."

"Son of a corpse eater. I'm going in there," said Benedict.

"Sir, that's not exactly a good idea," said Juma. "That way not only will they have the children as hostages, but they will have you."

"The entire 142$^{nd}$ knows my policy on hostages. We do everything possible to get them out, but we do not give into demands. If anything happens to me, Morales will do an exemplary job leading the 142$^{nd}$ Starborne. I am the only one that has a chance of ending this without bloodshed." He handed off his rifle and sidearm to the colonel and turned to the captain. "Monitor my frequency. I assume snipers are already in place?"

"Yes sir. Unfortunately, he has blocked off all the windows and has space heaters going to confuse infrared."

Benedict nodded. "I will have all the communications gear that is in my uniform on full sensor mode. That should be able to get them a pretty good picture of what is inside. Have them standing by with armor-piercing shells. They will be able to tell me apart from anybody else over three feet tall. The children are *not* acceptable losses. Is that understood?"

"Yes, sir."

Benedict spoke into his headset microphone. "Tie me into the Harpies' speaker systems." Benedict heard the squelch of the feedback. "Voice, this is Benedict. I'm coming in, I'm alone and I'm unarmed."

The vampire governor arrived on the scene and threw the

soldier that tried to stop him ten feet. A dozen more soldiers moved toward him. "Captain, explain to Governor Longstrum *exactly* what we are doing, but do not let him near the building. Hold our people back."

Already moving, Juma nodded. "Yes, sir."

Benedict was met at the door by one of Voice's men with a sidearm.

"Major, you've come to join us?"

"Why else would I be here?" Benedict had learned long ago that while it was best not to lie in negotiations, it was also best to say things that allow people to jump to their own satisfactory conclusion and not correct them when they are wrong. "Bring me to Voice."

Benedict's armed escort took him to the daycare center. "Hans, you have come to join us in our hour of victory."

Benedict noted that he was no longer "major." Voice had already in his mind assumed command of the planet and, instead of being an ally with all the cards, Benedict had now been demoted to support personnel.

"This will make those complacent humans pick up the fight against the vampire overlords. No more acceptance. They will have to open up their eyes and see the monsters for what they really are."

"Yes, that's definitely been accomplished. Everyone knows exactly who the monsters are now. The question is are you really prepared to harm these children?"

"Hans, I was in the Host, the same as you. We both had to do despicable, horrible things because we were ordered to. It was never pleasant; it was never good. Still, we did them because we were following orders, because we trusted in the long run it was for the greater good. I don't want to harm a hair on any of these kids' heads, however, I will do whatever is necessary to set my world free."

"An admirable viewpoint. However, you crossed the line when you took the innocent hostage."

"Innocent? They're not innocent. Their parents are conspirers. Already they're being indoctrinated to accept meekly the vampires as their betters. They are going to grow up to become nothing but sheep fit for the slaughter. Better they die here and now than as the meal for some monstrous bloodsucker."

"So you are the one who killed those people, making it look like a bloodsucker, right?"

Voice's eyebrows raised and the corner of his lips curled up. "I knew I wouldn't be able to fool you, but the rest of the population is another matter."

"Did you do it on your own? All six murders? Because that would have been very impressive for one man to pull off on his own," Benedict said.

"I would like to say I did, but every man in this room helped. It was a true team effort."

"How'd you choose the victims?"

"Each of us chose one person who we felt this world would be better off without. Most of them were criminals and the rest of us were better with them on the underside of a grave. So what do you think of my plan? Ingenious, huh? You think people will finally rise up and join us?"

"The people are absolutely about to rise up. In fact, we have taken the bloodsucking so-called governor into custody. As you said, what you did was quite ingenious, but you crossed the line with the children. I'm here to make you a deal. Longstrum is right outside that window. You let the children go and we will put a bullet in Longstrum's brainpan right now. Then you can go outside and lop off his head."

"Everyone will see?"

"I'm pretty sure all the news feeds are out there. It won't hurt your bid to become the new planetary governor,"

"I like the plan except for the part where I give up the hostages. We both know that the vampires are stronger and faster than us. Without these kids here, even we trained soldiers will be chopped meat."

"We can still put the bullet in his head, but you know he feeds regularly and often so if you're not down there quickly enough his body will spit out the bullet and heal. Might take a little bit for all the neurological damage to go away, but you don't want to waste time getting down there to lop off the head."

"It's not that I don't believe you, Benedict, it's just I don't trust anyone outside of my people. I'm going to take this girl and go over to the window. If you are on the level about this, then I'll let half of the kids go."

"No problem." Benedict hit a button on his collar. "This is Benedict. Please arrange the bloodsucker's execution so Mr. Voice can watch."

Voice moved to the window and pulled away a corner of the paper so he could see out. In the street below, the vampire governor was on his knees with his hands behind his head. Captain Juma looked up at the window to make sure that Voice could see him and he pulled his trigger. There was a loud bang and the vampire fell to the ground twitching.

Voice gave out a rebel yell, dropping to his knees and thrusting his arms in front of him. "The 142nd Starborne did it. They put a bullet in that bloodsucker's head!" He pushed the little girl away towards Benedict. "Take her and half the kids, Benedict. You're all right in my book."

Benedict knelt down so he was at eye level with the child. "Are you okay?" The girl nodded. Benedict grabbed her and pulled her close and whispered, "*Salt it.*" He threw the two of them down to the floor as armor-piercing rounds tore through the building, taking out all the terrorists except the still kneeling Voice with a headshot. Voice looked around and started to bring his weapon to bear on Benedict, but he was still reeling from the shock of seeing his fellows shot down and moved too slowly. Benedict had already slipped the ceramic knife out of the armored plating of his sleeve and tossed it so it went into Voice's throat so deep that it severed his spine. The gun fell from the rebel leader's hand and he fell to the ground.

A strike team was inside in moments and the children were taken out and reunited with their parents. When Benedict exited the building, the unharmed vampire governor was there to meet him.

"I was still thinking it had to be some kind of a trick up until I heard the shot and felt nothing."

"Thank you for trusting us. I'm still not crazy about the idea of vampires being in charge, but for this world you really do seem like the best option."

"So you won't be interfering in anything here?"

"Not at the moment. However, in my time here I have made some contacts and given them ways to contact us. I will be keeping an eye on you. Remember that. And make sure you keep these people safe."

The vampire nodded and began to extend his hand to shake Benedict's but stopped. Instead, he snapped to attention and saluted. Benedict matched the stance and saluted back before turning toward the nearest Harpy. His people could handle clean up. He had to figure out what else needed to be done out there.

# THE MACHINE
# IN THE GHOST

His eyes opened with a mechanical click and Ted Hugh woke screaming to visions of his flesh being dissolved and burned away in a pool of green.

"Nooo!"

"Soldier, get a hold of yourself. You're safe. You survived." A man in a major's uniform stood over Ted's hospital bed. The man wasn't especially tall, but he was fit, with graying hair at his temples. The first things Ted noticed were the man's eyes. They were hard and cold, yet somehow comforting. "At least in a manner of speaking. Private Hugh, what is the last thing you remember?"

It took Ted some effort to focus past the trauma of emerald acid eating away at his arms, legs, and even his face. He had to work not to flinch as the memories of the alien, amoeba-like creatures made him want to flee. He fought to maintain his position in bed.

"We were… We were fighting the globs, weren't we, sir?" The major nodded. "They were attacking one of the cattle yards on the eastern settlement. All the cows had been rounded up for Rushmore's annual butchering."

The creatures plummeted down from space inside fiery meteors. The heat of entry combined with the impact allowed the globs to break out of their rocky shells and attack the colony.

"They were relentless, but we held the line long enough

for the settlers to use their vehicles and horses to move the herds into some of our dropships. Once the animals were safe, we were given the order to bug out, but the dropships weren't there because they were transporting cattle. I held the rear and…" A vision of one of the gel-like aliens sprouting a tentacle and grabbing hold of his foot flooded his memory. He was dragged shooting and screaming inside the glob. Ted burned as if the flesh was still liquefying off his arms and legs.

"The globs got me, didn't they, Major?"

"They did, soldier. You would have died too, if not for the quick actions of Corporal Sato and Sergeant Mile."

Ted turned his neck to look at the two people stepping up to his bed. The movement seemed slow and heavy, like his spine had been injured. Sergeant Mile was a man of about thirty years with a buzz cut that showed more brown skin than brown hair on the top of his head, but Ted's attention focused primarily on the corporal. Sato  was maybe five-foot-four to the sergeant's six-two and Ted could not stop staring. The woman was absolutely beautiful, even in her black uniform with her hair tied up in a bun high on top of her head. Her Asian features seemed to be amazingly symmetrical and when she smiled it was all over for him.

"Thank you, but I'm sorry. You both seem familiar, but I don't remember you. Or you, Major."

"Understandable considering the trauma you've been through. The doctors have assured us your memories will return gradually. I suppose I should introduce myself. I'm Major Hans Benedict, commander of the 142$^{nd}$ Starborne."

"I remember the 142$^{nd}$ Starborne. I've served for over five years onboard the Colossus-class warship *Behemoth*.

"I better get back to duty." As Ted pushed himself up

from the bed his limbs felt odd, He looked down and saw metal where flesh should've been. A lot of metal.

"What the hell happened to my arm?" He looked at his other arm and then his legs. He realized his entire body was metal. He looked like a tank that had been melted down around a man with arms and legs that belonged on a dropship crane rather than a person. He was huge, wider, and taller than anyone he had ever met. "What happened to me?"

"I'm sorry, soldier. We airlifted you out, but the globs had done a number on you and eaten away most of the flesh on your limbs and much of your face. Mile and Sato got you out of the creature before it ate your organs. We were able to stabilize you, but there was no way for us to replace what was taken. The only way to save you was to make you a cyborg."

"Without asking me?"

"Soldier, when you were called to join the Host, you filled out the same paperwork the rest of us did. You checked the box authorizing the Host to save you in any way possible. One of those methods listed was cyborg. Your body is still inside that shell, but you can never leave it. You've been in a medically induced coma until you were stable."

"I'm a little achy, but I'm not really in much pain. Shouldn't I be in agony?"

"You should, but that's the beauty of nerve blocks. Very few of the sensory nerves you have left can transmit signals back to your brain. It's a blessing really."

"It's good to have you back, Ted," Corporal Sato said. When she smiled at him he got lost for a moment and everything else seemed to fade away.

"Yes, it's good to have you back," Sergeant Mile said, but

the man didn't look very happy.

"I'm just sorry we couldn't get to you sooner," Sato said.

"It was the globs' fault, not yours. You did the best you could, Lorna." Ted paused for a moment. "That's your first name, isn't it?"

Sato smiled again. "It is. Maybe your memories are coming back."

Mile rolled his eyes, then saw Benedict and smiled, but it seemed forced.

"I guess."

"I'm sure you have questions, so ask away," Major Benedict said.

There was something on Ted's mind, but he looked awkwardly at Lorna. "Would you two mind giving us a moment?"

"Sure, but I will wait outside for you. When you're done, I'll take you back to Medusa Squad's barracks," Lorna said.

"Thanks."

As soon as the sergeant and corporal left the room, Ted turned to Benedict. "Sir, did the Glob get everything?" Benedict raised his eyebrows. "I mean, did they get the important stuff." Ted pointed his metal hand at his groin.

Benedict's eyes widened in understanding, then softened. "Unfortunately, son, it did. They were just flesh and couldn't stand up to the acidic enzymes inside the glob. I'm sorry."

"Not as sorry as I am. Of that, I can assure you."

Benedict gave a sad chuckle. "I'm sure, but the doctors built a stress reliever function into your armor. Anytime you need to, you can plug into a jack over there and it'll send an electric impulse to the pleasure centers of your brain. It won't be the same as the physical act but it's something."

"Thank you, sir. How do I go to the bathroom? How do I eat?"

"Once every three days or so you'll have to change your nutrient and waste bags. All your internal plumbing is hooked up so you don't have to worry about going, especially since you lost the muscles that would assist with that. You'll just go whenever you have to. I've been assured the process is automatic and you'll barely notice."

Ted spent the next fifteen minutes asking more questions and was told to report first thing in the morning to learn how to use his new cyborg body.

"In the meantime, you go back to the barracks and get some rest."

"You mean I can still sleep?"

"Of course. Sleeping and dreaming is a very important safety valve. However, I've been told you can go without sleep for up to ten days without severe consequences. It'll come in handy if you have to take an extra watch so your squad can get some rest."

Major Hans saluted Private Ted Hugh who returned the salute, then rushed off, trying out his new body, excited to be able to spend time with Corporal Sato.

Private Hugh excelled throughout his retraining. He'd always been a good soldier but had never considered himself anything special. That had now changed. The basic training that lasted twelve weeks the first time took him less than five days to master. The surgeons had not just reconstructed his body, they improved his brain. It made sense for him to be stronger and faster with his cyborg battle armor, but his reaction time and ability to process the environment around him had improved tenfold. The battle armor's sensors let him see things a mile away or zoom in on something microscopic. Not only could he hear a whisper in the next room as clearly as if the person was standing next to him, but he could make out things in the ultrasonic range that normal human ears didn't even know existed. If the techs hadn't shown him the med scans of the ruined body beneath the armor, he wouldn't have believed there was any flesh still left there.

Another benefit was he had become a whiz at mathematics. Ted had always been decent with numbers, rarely ever needing a calculator for basic computations, but now the upgrades to his gray matter let him triangulate and aim his weapons like a computer. Better really, because not only did he have the speed and processing power of a machine, but the heart and mind of a man. It was the best of both worlds, except for the lack of most of his body. And not being able to feel. Actually, that wasn't true exactly. The battle-armor had touch receptors built in for deep and light touch. There were thermal receptors, others that measured the movement of air currents around him and ones that measured radio waves and radiation. It just wasn't the same as the way his body's old sense of touch.

He didn't understand it all. One night when visiting with Major Benedict, Ted asked, "How did they upgrade my brain just by hooking me up to a machine? I'm smarter and able to calculate things that only a genius or a computer should be able to. And if they can do it for me, why aren't they doing it for other soldiers? I asked the techs and they were evasive. One said he wasn't allowed to tell me. Should what I am really be classified and kept from me?"

"It's complicated, Ted," Benedict said.

"As I said, I'm very smart now. I think I'll understand it. But I don't understand why there are no other cyborgs like me in the 142$^{nd}$. I've seen a few cyborg soldiers with mechanical limbs or eyes, but nobody with my kind of body armor."

"Because the interface to your armor is one-of-a-kind technology we recovered when we were on Wutai. We were there to rescue William Cortner, a brilliant scientist."

Ted nodded his metal head. "Cortner made advances in human-machine interfaces beyond anything anyone had done before. He also managed to keep human brains alive outside of the body and hook them up to robots, not to mention make huge advances in robotic AI."

Benedict frowned. "How do you know all that?"

Ted shrugged his mechanical shoulders. "The techs had info about him on their screens during my last checkup. With my electronic eyes, I just need to glance at something to be able to read it."

Benedict nodded. "His work is still classified. And difficult to figure out. Unfortunately, Cortner… died. We salvaged much of his work and research, but it's taken us years to get it working well enough to use for soldiers like yourself."

"So I'm the first?"

Major Benedict hesitated. "You're the second."

"What happened to the first?"

"He couldn't cope with what he was and cracked under the strain. We made some changes in the interface for you and so far, it seems to be working."

"I guess. Better than dying at any rate," Ted said.

One night in the mess hall, Ted found himself

bemoaning the situation to Lorna Sato. It wasn't something he would normally share with a superior officer, but Lorna had turned into a friend. The best friend he'd had since his wife died during the extermination of humanity on Earth.

"Ted, there's no point in crying over dissolved body parts," Lorna replied.

It was rude, but the way she said it made him laugh, which he knew she had intended. Her upbeat attitude and inability to feel sorry for him was the main reason he went into the mess at mealtime. Not that he could eat. He was told that some of his digestive tract survived, but there had been too much trauma for it to process regular food. The only nourishment he got was dripped in through his nutrient bag.

It wasn't easy being a mechanical man, particularly at mealtime. For the first week or so he sat at a table with the rest of Medusa Squad, but it was obvious most of them felt uneasy around him. They greeted him but didn't offer much in the way of small talk or conversation. Ted understood. He wasn't the same man he used to be and, outside of squad business, he didn't really have much in common with them anymore. It's not like he could ask them if they had any tricks to make changing a waste bag easier.

Gradually, his fellow soldiers drifted away to sit at another table. Occasionally Sergeant Mile would join him for a meal, but it seemed more out of a sense of duty rather than any real desire for Ted's company. Only Lorna never went to the other table and so he always came to mess to spend time with her.

She was understanding and never judged. Lorna reminded him of Aimee with her kindness. Ted still missed his wife and their kids, Sheela and Danny. The techs had downloaded his pictures of them into his armor's storage so he could look at them whenever he liked.

He put a family pic on his wrist com and showed Lorna.

"This is my favorite. It's the four of us the last time I had leave on Earth."

"You all look so happy," Lorna said.

"We were." It bothered Ted that the armor's speakers didn't carry the emotion in his voice or the sigh he made. "Sheela was six and Danny four. Aimee and I had such a wonderful reunion that child number three was on the way before I shipped back out. It would have been a girl."

"I'm sorry. Did you have a name picked out?"

"Yes. Lucy."

"Pretty."

"She would have been, just like Sheela and their mother. Now my family is nothing but ashes light years away."

"Mine too."

It turned out that Ted and Lorna had more than that in common. They both came from broken homes with alcoholic parents. Each one of them ended up doing more to raise their siblings than either their mother or father. And despite it all, they both missed their parents now that Earth was decimated.

"I guess when you look at it, we're the lucky ones," she said.

"I'm not too sure I'd call myself lucky."

"I call bullshit. You're here. You exist. The people back on Earth don't," she said.

"So you don't believe in heaven or an afterlife?"

"Actually, I do. I was raised Shinto."

"Isn't that the religion which believes that every rock and tree has a spirit or soul?"

"That's an overly simplistic explanation of kami, but not entirely wrong. I believe that every living thing has a spirit and I don't believe that that spirit ceases to be just because the vessel holding it does. I like to believe there is a heaven of some sort, a place we go when we die that's much better than this universe. That we're rewarded for our deeds."

"What about punished for sins?" Ted said.

Lorna shrugged. "I'm not that obsessed about balancing scales or revenge for wrongdoing. I just like to think that we all go to a better place where we will be better people."

"I like that a lot. That means someday I'll see Aimee, Danny, and Sheela again. And finally get to meet little Lucy."

Lorna smiled and put her hand over the back of Ted's metal one. For an instant, he swore he could feel her touch the way he felt things *before* an alien devoured most of his body.


On Tuesday nights there was an inter-unit basketball game onboard *Behemoth*. Ted hadn't been much of a basketball player pre-cyborg. He was more of a baseball guy, but he'd come to appreciate the nuances of the game, although it wasn't exactly fair when he played. In his battle armor, he stood eight feet tall with plating that could withstand shell blasts. He was also as strong as a tank. Originally the other units tried to ban him from the game, but Major Hans Benedict wouldn't hear of it. He told the soldiers to think of it as a challenge. However, Benedict did allow them to make special rules for Ted—he was limited to standing in an eight-foot circle just outside the three-point line for his team's home basket and couldn't hold onto the ball for more than three seconds. Thanks to his cybernetic enhancements, three seconds might as well have been a minute. Ted could consistently sink a shot across the court using the same calculating power he would use to fire any of the weapons built into his armor, which is why they only allowed him to use one hand. Without extending the metal, his hands could still reach almost twelve feet up in the air, so he was easy to pass to. He did his best to simply throw the ball to his teammates, only taking the occasional shot. One time the opposing team had fouled him and they had to go for a jump shot. Ted's feet never left the floor, but he did manage to shoot the ball directly into the basket.

Even the opposing team clapped when he made that one.

It was the first time he felt like he belonged, outside of meals with Lorna.


Ted slept in the barracks with the rest of the soldiers, men and women alike. The main difference was his bed was larger and better reinforced.

Ted didn't quite fall asleep as easily as he did before he got his battle-armor. Then he just drifted off to sleep. Now he had to make a conscious effort, but it wasn't too difficult. Usually. That night was different. In the morning they were going planetside. Seems a new batch of globs had gotten past the *Behemoth's* and Rushmore's orbital defense system and were harassing the locals. Medusa Squad would be relieving Euryale Squad on the ground.

Ted didn't want to admit it, even within the quiet reaches of his mind, but he was scared. Logically, he knew that his battle armor was tough enough that it would take a gargantuan glob to hurt him now, and nothing of that size had shown up on Rushmore so far.

Ted was still afraid. This would be his first time in the field since the accident and he didn't want to let his fellow soldiers down. Or Sergeant Mile or Major Benedict. Most importantly he didn't want to disappoint Lorna. Ted knew he was falling in love with her. At first, it felt like he was betraying Aimee and the kids, but Ted knew in his heart that Aimee would be okay with it. She had wanted his happiness above her own, which is why she'd let him enlist in the first place—it was what he'd wanted and Aimee had always been so afraid he wouldn't come back to her. The irony of what had happened didn't escape him. Besides, she had the same bitterly sardonic sense of humor as Lorna. She'd point out that even if they became involved, he couldn't sleep with Lorna even if they both wanted to, so he wasn't technically cheating on her.

Ted suspected Lorna had feelings for him too, but it was pointless. He was stuck inside a giant tin can. He couldn't offer Lorna a real relationship. There was no chance of physical intimacy. Not even for a real kiss. Even if there was a way to remove his helmet, his face was hideous and his lips had been dissolved. The doctors had let him see the scans of what was left of his body. Recalling an old Irish war song, he realized he was an eyeless, boneless, chickenless egg. If not for the battle armor, he'd be dead. At least this way, he could still be a good soldier. Ted could protect civilians and his fellow soldiers. It wasn't the life he would have chosen, but he could still do something positive with it. He just had to ignore the hurt in his heart.

Ted turned his head to look across the barracks where

Medusa Squad slept. He bunked in the center with the privates and Lorna was closer to the wall because of her rank. Like most of the soldiers, she slept in shorts and a tank top with nothing beneath it. Lorna lay on her side facing his side of the room, her blanket crumpled down by her legs. Because it was lights out, Ted automatically shifted his vision into infrared mode. Despite the distance, he could see Lorna as clearly as if he were standing next to her. Ted smiled as he watched her sleep. It took him a moment to realize that with the infrared on, he could see her body heat seep through her clothing and it showed up on his sensors as if she were naked. Being a decent guy, Ted quickly turned his head away, but the image of her beautiful body had burned itself into his memory as clearly as if he had taken a picture. Ted was soon obsessing over the visual. He tried to think of the mission, basketball, or anything else, and when that didn't work he forced himself to focus and induce sleep

Ted slept and the dreams that came in that undiscovered country were of a decidedly carnal nature. He was whole again—man, not machine—and that was how he came to Lorna. They reached out toward each other and together they did the things that men and women who hold both love and lust for each other will do. And for the first time since the accident, Ted was happy.

Ted awoke with a phantom limb sensation in his groin. It wasn't a pain, but more of a throbbing and a longing. He realized that he was not alone so he covered himself with his hands, then moved them away when he realized there was no need to cover a part he no longer laid claim to. Try as he might, Ted could not fall back to sleep. When he found himself again staring at Lorna, Ted got up and went to the medical room where he had awoken. He stood in front of the machine that Major Benedict told him about. Ted had not tried it yet, but now he felt a burning need that had no other release. Opening the control panel on the side of his rib cage, Ted connected a cable from the device to his chest. He couldn't get the vision of Lorna under infrared out of his mind, so instead he imagined her looking into his real eyes as he pushed the button.

Ted's brain exploded and tingled with all kinds of wonderful sensations. For a minute or more what remained of his body flooded with ecstasy and what endured of his flesh convulsed like it had with Aimee when he was a real man. When it was done, his stress was gone, released from his body and mind in one blissful burst. It wasn't as good as it had been when he still had his original parts, but it helped.

Ted wanted to do it again, but there was a once-a-day limit to prevent addiction. After all, he wouldn't do the 142$^{nd}$ Starborne any good plugged into the medical lab and pushing the button all day. Instead, he went to a view room and stared at the planet below and the stars above until the morning.

"Do understand your orders, Private Hugh?"

"Yes, Sergeant. You want me to carry the rest of you and do all the work. Guess it's my fault for lounging around so much since my accident." In Ted's mind, he was smiling, but he couldn't be sure if his face was doing the same. Unfortunately, he was sure the battle armor's face was still an unmoving mask.

Sergeant Mile frowned.

"Take it easy on the Sarge, Ted. You know he doesn't have a sense of humor," Corporal Sato said as she gently touched Ted on his encased elbow. "Don't get cocky just because you're in that tank. You be careful."

Ted's unseen, but intently felt smile grew larger at the small gesture of caring. "Yes, ma'am."

The Harpy dropship would deposit them near the relocated herd. Or at least part of it. To reduce the risk of the globs devouring the livestock, the animals were split into smaller groups, delivering only as many cattle to the slaughterhouse that could be butchered during that day. They were working round-the-clock in an attempt to finish the annual butchering and preserving the meat before the globs could get hold of the animals.

Medusa squad's mission was to protect the portion of the herd awaiting butchering.

Ted had his own drop point, five miles away where a gaggle of twenty globs was on an intercept course with the herd, oozing their way across the landscape, leaving trails of barren earth behind them.

Private Hugh was deposited half a mile ahead of the gaggle. It was his mission to destroy the globs before they got to the herd. Ted walked down the landing ramp and waved as the Harpy dropship took off, wishing he could wink at Lorna. The rest of Medusa Squad would form a defensive perimeter and pick off any globs that got past Ted.

Killing a glob wasn't easy. Energy weapons only made matters worse. The globs' resistance to intense heat allowed them to survive entry into the planet's atmosphere. Instead of boiling them away, they were able to channel the discharge from the energy weapons and grow bigger, which in turn made them hungrier. Small projectile weapons bounced off their outer membrane. Larger and higher velocity projectile weapons only made holes that healed quickly. The 142$^{nd}$ Starborne had developed special, armor-piercing rounds filled with a variation of francium hydroxide, a highly concentrated base that interacted with the globs' natural acidity and destroyed them much the same way slugs on Earth died when salt was poured on top of them. The rounds had to be shielded because of the radiation the formula gave off.

Even with the special rounds, it still took upward of a dozen shots penetrating the membrane to wound even a small glob. The medium and larger ones could shrug the rounds off and their outer membranes were tough enough to protect the creatures when the formula was dropped directly on them. Rocket launchers helped.

Private Hugh, however, had arm cannons, able to fire 32-mm rounds filled with the formula. One round would take out even a large glob and make the smaller ones expand so quickly that their membranes blew up like a balloon filled with baking soda and vinegar. Thanks to his battle armor, Ted was strong enough to carry what amounted to a backpack ammo clip that carried three hundred and fifty of the large rounds. He also had a tank filled with the formula that he could propel like a hose through a finger in each hand.

Ted walked with slow, measured paces in the direction of the gaggle. He wanted to run to get there faster, to prove himself worthy of all the effort the 142$^{nd}$ Starborne had put into saving him, but he didn't. It was more important to make sure every last glob was taken out. Plus, he was more than a little nervous. He was worried that if he rushed his mission one or more globs would get by him and hurt the rest of his squad.

Using the enhanced visual sensors built into his battle armor Ted calculated the spot closest to the center of the gaggle, tore open a vacuum-sealed package, and threw a pair of bull legs toward the globs. The meat landed one hundred feet away.

Using a methodology from an old hunting practice known as baiting, the scent of fresh meat and blood was supposed to draw all the globs toward the meat. The tacticians onboard *Behemoth* theorized that since Ted's human bits were encased within the bio armor he should be practically invisible to the globs. That would change once he opened fire.

Ted extended his arm cannons and waited. The globs moved by extending part of their membrane forward and contracting the rest of it in, like an amoeba. The best way Ted could describe it was as a rapid ooze.

The first glob reached the raw beef. A second joined it not long after. Ted held his fire until five of the twenty were at the bait pile and the rest were fairly close by. His first targets were the ones furthest away, figuring those would be the ones most likely to escape. The first shot was dead on, but he missed the second. Ted realized he'd forgotten to compensate for the wind currents and his next five shots hit their targets.

The outermost six globs' insides turned from green to white as the creatures fizzled and died. Two exploded outward from the pressure caused by the chemical reaction.

The rest of the gaggle didn't ignore the attack. One managed to launch itself at him, flying through the air to land on his helmet.

Ted froze. In that instant, he was suddenly flesh and

bone again, back inside the creature that almost killed him. He was so traumatized by the flashback that he didn't realize that three more globs had grabbed hold of him and were trying to dissolve his hard armor casing to get at the fleshy human center.

His salvation came in the form of an angel over his communicator. "Ted, this is Lorna. Have you engaged the enemy?"

Her voice brought him back to the present. Before he answered Ted turned on his finger hoses. They were designed to use water or other chemicals to control a fire or an unruly crowd. The globs trying to dissolve his arms had already let the battle armor inside their membranes, so he let loose a spray of the francium hydroxide solution. The pair became white and he was able to shake their lifeless forms off his arms. Next, he maneuvered a finger between his arm and the one that was on his head. Once it was past the membrane he sprayed the formula inside and it too blanched and died. A glob at his foot realized something was wrong and fled, but he managed to put two rounds into it.

"I have engaged the enemy. Half are down, ten to go."

"Good job. I knew you could do it."

A voice Ted recognized as Captain Shana Morales, the 142nd's second in command broke in over the comm channel. "Medusa Squad, we have another incoming breaking orbit. We launched a missile at it, but it shrugged it off. Judging by its size, this will be the biggest glob to make planetfall on Rushmore and it's headed toward you. It will land less than two miles northwest of your herd. Evacuate immediately. Get the herd and the butchers out of there. The blood in the slaughterhouse will act as a beacon to this thing."

"Captain Morales, this is Private Hugh. Should I join the rest of Medusa?"

"Negative, Hugh. Complete your mission first before rejoining Medusa Squad."

"Acknowledged."

Private Hugh fired at the remaining gaggle but was distracted by worrying about the rest of his squad and only made seven of the ten shots. He still found it awkward to think in order to fire a weapon instead of pulling a trigger.

Above him, a fiery boulder, bigger than a dropship, raced toward the planet and landed a few miles away. Its impact shook the ground even where he was standing. His next two shots hit their targets, but the sole surviving member of the gaggle launched itself away, toward where the meteor had landed. It leapt three more times and then was apparently unable to do it again so resumed oozing forward.

Running all out, Private Hugh could attain speeds of eighty miles per hour. It did not take him long to overtake and shoot the last glob. His mission completed, Ted sped up, pushing himself to his limits and exceeding what the maximum speed of the battle armor was supposed to be able to do by almost six miles an hour.

"Medusa Squad, this is Hugh. Mission is complete. I'm en route to your location. What is your situation?"

"Situation is FUBAR," Sergeant Mile said. "This glob is gargantuan. It's easily a hundred and twenty feet in diameter and thirty feet high. It's moving faster than the herd is able to travel." Sounds of rapid-fire weapons going off came over the channel. "It shrugs off our armor-piercing rounds. Our rockets are getting through but having zero effect. We need airlifts for the cattle."

"Negative, we don't have enough dropships available to

even get half the herd out. Without that meat, thousands will starve. Hold your position," Morales said.

A new voice broke in on the channel. "Captain Morales, this is Lieutenant Patel. I'm piloting Harpy Alpha Nine. I have four barrels of formula on board. If I kamikaze the dropship at the gargantuan glob, the impact will get the ship and the barrels past the membrane, it should be enough to destroy it."

"Lieutenant Patel, this is Major Benedict. What you're proposing is suicide."

"Yes, sir, but if we do nothing our soldiers and the herd will be dead," she said. "If I do this, our people survive. The herd survives and so do the people of Rushmore. I will try to eject before impact."

"The glob would gobble you up before you hit the ground. There has to be a better way," Major Benedict said.

"Major Benedict, this is Private Hugh. I think I have that better way. If Harpy Alpha Nine picks me up, we can attach the barrels to my battle armor and drop me from a high altitude. Hopefully, my velocity will allow me to break through the membrane and destroy this creature, saving both the dropship and Lieutenant Patel."

There was a small gasp on the channel which Ted recognized as Lorna.

"Private, you do realize it's still a suicide mission."

"Yes, sir, but I should've died the first time the globs got me. I'll be damned if I let them get anyone else when I can stop them. Let me even the score, sir. It won't get my body back, but I'll take out the bastards' biggest threat."

"Your bravery is to be commended, Private Hugh. Lieutenant Patel, rendezvous with Private Hugh and enact his plan."

"Yes, sir."

"Better hurry, Hugh," Mile said. "I doubt we have fifteen minutes."

"Don't worry, Sarge. I'll get there in time. I told you I'd do all the work."

Patel had the landing ramp open before she reached him. Ted's battle armor allowed him to leap high enough that she didn't need to touch ground.

"I'm on board, Patel. Go!"

The Harpy crew used cables to string the four barrels to Ted's back.

"I'm planning to get to thirty-five hundred feet above that monster," Patel said.

"Hugh, this is Morales. Your impact alone may not be enough to break the giant's membrane. You need to fire at it continuously once you hit the seven-hundred-foot mark, to soften it up to make sure you get through with your payload. Any questions?"

"Just one—how do I get the formula out of the barrels? Do I need to save four rounds?"

"Even in your armor, there's no guarantee you're going to survive the impact and be able to do that. Fortunately for the mission, you won't have to. The acid in that thing's gullet will eat through the barrels in a couple of seconds and give it a case of terminal indigestion."

Ted nodded, then realized Morales couldn't see him. "Yes, ma'am."

"We'll be in position in ninety seconds," Patel said.

Private Hugh gave the pilot a thumbs up and let the knowledge that he was about to make a suicide jump sink in. His parents, his wife, and his kids had all died on Earth long before he was turned into a machine. He'd never gotten over the loss but had come to terms with it. There really was only one person left alive that he wanted to say goodbye to.

Ted opened a private channel. "Lorna."

"Yes, Ted?" Was that a tremor in her voice? Was she holding back tears? Ted knew he was and had been impressed that his voice hadn't cracked, even through his mechanical filter.

"I just wanted to say goodbye and thank you. What happened to me after the glob attack was not easy, but you made it bearable. I just wanted to let you know that you mean something to me."

"Ted, you mean a lot…"

"Private, you are over the drop zone," cut in Lieutenant Patel. "That monster is moving fast. You need to jump, now."

"Roger that, Lieutenant. Goodbye, Lorna."

If Ted was going to go out, he was going to go out in style. Ted strutted up to the edge of the open ramp and dove like he would into a pool, flipping himself twice in the air.

"Ted!" Lorna's voice echoed in his ear until it was cut off.

The world became strangely peaceful as the air rushed past him. Ted had plenty of time to twist his body so that he was plummeting to face the creature with his hands and arm cannons leading the way.

Lieutenant Patel hadn't been entirely accurate in her description of their position. The Harpy wasn't exactly over the colossal glob, but in the position above where it would be by the time Ted hit the ground. There was always a chance that the calculations were wrong and he would miss, but Lieutenant Patel's math was double-checked by both Major Benedict and Ted himself. The same error at the ten-thousandth decimal point was found by both Benedict and Ted so adjustments were made to assure he would hit the center and not the tail-end of the creature.

"Private Hugh, you are at the seven-hundred-foot mark. Fire at will," Lieutenant Patel said.

It was amazing how much he could take in as he started firing at his point of impact. Ted could not only see the huge glob but a smaller gaggle of four making its way toward Medusa Squad. He was in the zone like never before. With his left hand, Ted took aim, accounting for velocity, wind, his rate of descent, and a dozen other minute factors, and fired one test round.

It hit the colossal glob center mass. Ted smiled and used his enhanced vision to pick out Lorna from among the soldiers on the ground. Even though he must've appeared to be a dot in the sky to her, she looked up, smiled, and gave him a wave, realizing he'd be able to see her. He had started firing with both arms at the giant creature, so he simply nodded back at her. It's not like she could make out either gesture at this distance, but it made him smile.

The best scientists of the Sway government had only a rudimentary understanding of the glob sensory organs, but they were known to be able to sense vibration, heat, and blood better than sharks underwater and were somehow able to tell the difference between flesh and inorganic material.

From Ted's viewpoint, it seemed as if the colossal glob had no idea where the attack was coming from and it had stopped moving in an effort to pinpoint it. This made his job easier.

Instinct took over an instant before impact as Ted stopped firing and brought his arms up to protect his head. He felt metal crunch but the combination of velocity and a hundred-plus, formula-filled, armor-piercing rounds had done their work. Ted plunged deep into the gullet of the beast. The impact broke one of his mechanical arms off below the elbow and sensors began blaring that his outer shell had been breached by the acidic fluid. Ted took a deep breath of recycled air, released what was left in his finger spray tanks, and floated satisfied. He'd almost died inside a glob once. It seemed appropriate for him to meet his end the same way. He was just glad the big one was checking out with him and that his death would save Lorna and many other lives.

Less than fifteen seconds had passed since impact and he'd already lost his legs in addition to the rest of his left arm. Then the alarms stopped. Instead of the green acidic fluid, his sensors showed that he was now surrounded by white. A few heartbeats later he was thrown outward as the membrane ruptured from the internal pressure.

Ted's lungs shut down and he stopped breathing. The incessant background noise of his heart beating had ceased on his way out of the now-defunct glob.

His sensor screen flickered and began to fade until he caught a glimpse of Corporal Lorna Sato running toward him. Through sheer force of will, he made it stay on.

"Ted, are you still with us?"

"Barely, but not for much longer I think."

Sergeant Mile walked up behind Corporal Sato, put his hand on her shoulder, and pulled her back. "Sparky's done. We have globs on the ground. Leave him for scrap."

For the first time in his career, Ted wanted to strike a

superior officer. "Mile, you cold bastard. This is the second time I've saved your life."

"No, it's the first. The real Private Theodore Hugh died. He was killed by globs. They just created fake memories inside your head to make you think you were him so in case you checked, there would be records of your non-existent life. You don't even have the man's memories, just something a bunch of coders cooked up in a lab."

"Sergeant, shut the hell up and show some respect," Lorna yelled.

"For what? A machine? He did his job. He doesn't get any more thanks for that than my gun gets for firing. Asinine for them to make an AI think it's a cyborg because some lab rat figured it gives it some humanity and will make it a better soldier. And so it doesn't go batshit crazy like the other one. It is not, nor has it ever been, my job to babysit a toaster."

"I call bullshit!" Ted screamed somehow, even though the battle armor had shut down his breathing functions.

"Is it? The impact with the glob opened up your chest case. Okay, Private Cyborg, where the hell is your body?"

Ted lifted his head up to look at his open rib cage and stared at the lack of any human parts. The only thing organic was the contents of the food and waste bags and the tube connecting one to the other.

"How can this be possible? I can think. I remember. I had a childhood. I had parents, siblings, friends, a wife and kids who I loved and who loved me back. How can my entire life be a lie?" A light on his head started to blink rapidly and turned red.

"He's fading," Corporal Lorna Sato said.

"I told you to get back on duty."

"There are only three globs left and the rest of the squad has it managed." Corporal Sato pushed her superior officer back and pressed her earpiece. "Private Hugh is still with us, but not for long. We need immediate evac."

"This is Patel. Will be there in two minutes."

Private Hugh lost consciousness as they used a crane from the Harpy to load him on board.

There was a tunnel of light and Ted wondered if he'd see his family, then remembered they'd never existed. Instead, he opened his eyes. No, he didn't have eyes he corrected himself. Some sort of sensor array had turned on.

Ted was in a bed; the same one he'd woke up in after the glob attack. Or thought he had. He wasn't sure what was real anymore.

Lorna sat by his side. He prayed she was real.

"Hey." Her smile was as radiant as ever.

"Hey."

Lorna's hand gently touched the side of his metal cheek.

"Major Benedict, sir, he's awake," someone in a lab coat said.

Benedict came into view, standing over Ted's bedside. "Good work, Private. You did it. That section of the herd was successfully butchered, the meat preserved, and now awaiting distribution to the settlers. Another few days and we will have all the globs planetside wiped out and the settlers will be able to process the rest of the herd in safety. Thanks to your bravery and self-sacrifice, the people of Rushmore will make it through another year."

"I'm happy to hear that, sir, but I need to hear the truth."

Major Benedict nodded. "Your brain is too different and far more complex than any other system on the ship. It does have some organic components. We have nothing comparable to back up your mind to or we would. Cortner is the only one who might have known, but the fallen genius isn't talking. We tried our damnedest, but the truth is we're unable to save you. Ted, you're going to die."

"But if I'm not a man, was I ever alive? And if I wasn't alive, how can I die? Has my entire existence been a lie? What am I, sir?"

"What you are, Private Ted Hugh, is a soldier and a damn fine one at that. One of the finest soldiers I have ever had the privilege to have under my command. It has been said that there is no greater love than to give one's life for one's friends and comrades. After what you did down on Rushmore, you proved you have love in spades. And if you have love, as far as I'm concerned you are as much person as you are machine."

Ted looked at Lorna. "But if I'm not a man, I have no soul. I won't go to heaven."

"I call bullshit. If animals, mountains, and storms have kami, I guarantee you do too, Ted. And your spirit has more than earned a place in any heaven," Lorna said, kissing the side of his metal faceplate.

Major Benedict took out a medal and held it in front of Ted's electric eyes. "The Purple Heart has a long and proud tradition and you have more than earned it, soldier."

Major Benedict bent over 7and used a magnet to attach it to a portion of the right chest casing that still survived, as no pin would have done the job.

The red light on Private Ted Hugh's face began to flash like a strobe. It was a sure sign that his last moment swiftly approached.

Major Benedict nodded and Corporal Lorna Sato hit a button, raising the bed so Ted sat upright.

"Company salute!"

The mechanical head looked at the two dozen assembled soldiers of all ranks saluting him, then turned to see Lorna and Major Benedict standing alongside of them and doing the same. A quiet sob escaped the speakers as Private Ted Hugh lifted his remaining hand to his head and returned the salute. As the red strobe became a solid light, Private Hugh's arm dropped to the bed and his head lulled to the side as his light went out forever.

Lorna lowered the bed and gently pulled the sheet over the metal head.

The assembled soldiers stood a moment in respectful silence, then moved to resume their duties as people in lab coats took care of the fallen metal soldier and salvaged what they could.

"Mile, Sato, walk with me," Major Benedict said, leaving the lab. Sergeant Mile ran up alongside him and saluted. Major Benedict did not return the salute, just nodded for him to put his arm down. Sato walked slowly behind them, wiping tears from her eyes.

"Major, I want to file a report of insubordination in the field against Corporal Sato. I gave her a direct order multiple times, which she ignored."

"You mean the order for her to abandon a wounded fellow soldier to stand guard against a threat that others had in hand?"

"With all due respect, sir, it wasn't a soldier. It was a machine."

"And that's where you're wrong, Private Mile."

Mile stopped walking. "Sir, my rank is sergeant."

"Not anymore, Private Mile. Lorna here is a sergeant."

Lorna's face made one of the smiles which had made Ted's virtual heart skip a beat. "Thank you, sir." She saluted and Benedict returned this one.

"You're welcome, Sato."

Mile's face became a dark shade of red. "This is bullshit."

Major Hans Benedict slowly turned his face to Private Mile and frowned.

Mile swiftly paled as he realized what he had done. "Sorry, sir."

"Too little, too late. Report to the Harpy bay. They're going down to Rushmore on cleanup duty. The remains of the giant glob need to be contained and removed to protect the settlers. Pick up a biohazard suit and report for duty in one hour."

"Yes, sir." Private Mile double-timed his way out.

"Major Benedict, will we be holding a service for Private Hugh?"

"Of course. Would you give the eulogy, Sergeant Sato?"

She nodded. "It would be an honor, sir."

# STRAY SHOT

"What good is a sensor if there are so many ways to trick it?" Corporal Louise Harpole asked. It wasn't the first time the defuser had started this conversation and likely wouldn't be the last. It just helped take her mind off the danger involved in her job.

Sergeant Dartanian Cooper grinned as he petted a large, golden dog. "People may be able to fool sensors, but nothing fools old Blue here. Right, boy?"

The dog barked and nodded his head.

"Despite all my time with Blue, I still can't believe how intelligent the Host Canine Corps is," Corporal Harpole said.

"Shows what a century of selective breeding and genetic engineering can accomplish."

"I don't see how you're taking all this so easily. Planetary Governor Cross is a sick bastard."

Cooper shrugged. "Slick too. He's not the only mouse to play when the cats flew back to Earth." Cross had tried to turn himself into a dictator after his Host military contingent pulled out. Many of the other folks on Kilimanjaro tried to stop him, so Cross responded by taking the colony's children hostage during the school day. "The rebels sent out a distress call and the 142$^{nd}$ Starborne came to the rescue."

"You mean the three of us came. Most of the 142$^{nd}$ is still waiting somewhere safe," Harpole said, the corners of her eyes crinkling up.

"We are the first wave of the rescue since we are most

qualified to find out which bunkers Cross hid the kids in, not to mention find and dismantle the explosives. A real shame that all the *Behemoth's* sensors can't measure up to the nose of one good dog."

Blue made a sound that was more laugh than bark.

"Cross hiding behind non-combatants just soaks my biscuits in hot sauce, but I've got to grin and swallow like my Aunt Suzie made 'em."

"I don't even know what that means," Harpole said.

"Blue picks up on what I put out. I get angry or upset, so does he and he won't be at his best to sniff you out some bombs to defuse," Copper said.

"Assuming we have the right place. Last two targets we found nothing," Harpole said.

"Well you know what they say—third time's the charm. I just think it's funny that Benedict holds back the rest of the troops and lets the three of us take point."

Harpole shrugged. "Defusers are used to working alone. Don't make no sense to risk a hundred lives when you only have to risk one. Or three in this case. We need Blue to find the explosives, me to defuse the detonators, and you to look pretty."

Blue did his cross between a laugh and bark again. Twice.

"Don't hate me because I'm the best-looking in this bunch." Cooper made a show of looking between the woman and the dog. "Not that it's a big accomplishment in this motley crew."

Blue whimpered like his feelings were hurt. "Come on, you know you're the best-looking dog I know." Cooper bent over and took the lead off the 120-pound dog. "Okay boy, it's up to you. Go find those bombs so Louise here can turn them off and we can get those kids out. If they're here, that is."

Blue barked and nodded again, then proceeded to start sniffing the entrance to the underground tunnel. Although the planet Kilimanjaro was able to support human life, the surface tended to be hostile during much of the year, so most of the colony's settlements were built underground. The entire planet was littered with tunnels and bunkers, which made the task of finding a planet-full of kidnapped children a tough one.

The 142$^{nd}$ Starborne's ship *Behemoth,* the last known Colossus-class warship, had received no less than seventeen distress calls, each from a different rebel faction. Apparently, Cross's governing style involved pitting different factions against each other so they fought among themselves more than they did him. Their forces were divided so sharply that they couldn't put aside their differences long enough to organize an attack or rescue.

When the 142$^{nd}$ Starborne arrived in orbit, Cross first tried to negotiate. He had a lot of loyal troops between him and danger and assumed he had plenty of wiggle room. To his surprise Major Hans Benedict offered only one deal— let the children go and live. Or don't and die.

Cross ignored it, perhaps assuming that the man threatening him would never get past all of his soldiers or was bluffing. It might have worked if the local military had either the firepower or the training of the Host. It took less than an hour for the 142$^{nd}$ to take the governor's mansion.

Benedict didn't kill Cross outright. At first, he opted for a flesh wound to give him a chance to rethink taking the deal. The negotiating technique didn't impress Cross and he told Benedict to go screw himself.

Since physical pain hadn't loosened Cross's tongue, Benedict switched tactics to a truth serum. He had not used it as a first option because it had a nasty side effect of killing twelve percent of the people it was given to.

Unfortunately, Cross fell into that percentage and was reduced to a drooling idiot who died moments later. Benedict kept his corpse on ice in case they needed DNA, fingerprints, retina scans, or the like to defuse a bomb. So far they hadn't.

That left the 142$^{nd}$ Starborne with the Herculean task of searching an entire planet to find the children before their food and water ran out.

Many of the bunkers were built to military specs, which is why orbital sensors were useless. Even the use of Harpy dropships had been only minimally effective. Taking advantage of local intelligence and the capture of many of Cross's collaborators, they'd found several bunkers holding thousands of children, but the bean counters' best guess was they had only rescued seventy-two percent of those missing. That left far too many kids unaccounted for.

Blue stopped and froze, pointing his nose at one particular wall panel. The "imitating a statue" was part of canine corps training as some explosive devices were triggered by movement. Remaining still was a safer way to notify the bomb tech than barking.

Corporal Harpole walked over and whispered, "Good boy, Blue."

Cooper used a hand signal and the dog unfroze and went to his side. Harpole used a multi-tool from her vest to remove the panel, revealing two blocks of industrial-grade Z-5 explosive hooked up to a system of wires. Harpole made a gun signal with her hand to let Cooper and Blue know it was a live bomb. Her multi-spectrum goggles allowed her to see the power flow through the system and other things not visible to the unaided human eye.

Although it was against regulations, Cooper moved closer to watch Harpole at work. He wasn't certified as a bomb technician but had learned the basics and then some. One never knew when he might be called upon to help. Or worse, finish the job if something happened to Harpole. Both soldiers were so engrossed in the diffusing process that they didn't notice a wall panel at the far end of the corridor slide open and three soldiers wearing planetary colors step out with their weapons drawn—modern scatterguns, perfect for tunnel fighting. On the other paw, Blue did see them. The canine soldier leapt forward, knocking both humans to the ground an instant before a round would've hit them. It hit Blue instead. His canine body armor deflected the bulk of it, but the angle allowed some of the pellets to penetrate the gaps. The dog collapsed to the floor.

Both human members of the Host returned fire, dropping the soldier who had made the shot on Blue.

"Drop your weapons and surrender," Sergeant Cooper shouted.

"No, you drop your weapons," said one of the planetary soldiers. "We outnumber you."

Both members of the 142$^{nd}$ Starborne could see there were more soldiers behind the opening in the wall.

Corporal Harpole turned her persuader rifle and aimed at the Z-5. "You shoot me and I blow us all back to Earth."

"What are you talking about?"

"Cross lined this place with explosives to keep the rebels from trying to rescue their kids. Anything goes wrong and the whole bunker goes."

"Bullshit."

"She's not bluffing. Use your scopes to look at what was behind that panel," Cooper said. "Even if you drop us, she'll get the shot off, which will trigger a chain reaction that'll bring this place down on all our heads. Or maybe one of you will miss and do it for us."

The soldier looked through his scope and the blood drained from his face. "Oh shit."

"All of you come out of there. Put your safeties on and slide your weapons to me. Then put your hands on your head," Cooper ordered.

The eight planetary soldiers who were still upright obeyed with one exception. A man who looked to be in his fifties and bearing the rank of captain bent to treat the wounded man.

"You're a medic?" Cooper said.

"Doctor. The governor assigned me here in case anything happened to the children."

"Fine, you can tend to your injured after you work on our wounded," Cooper said.

"Wounded? That's a dog. This is a man."

"What's your name, Doc?"

"Wilmer."

"Well, Dr. Wilmer, that dog is a soldier of the Host and my partner. He is also our only shot to find all the explosives and keep everyone in here alive," he said.

"That's fine, but I'm taking care of Jonesy first."

Cooper stood then walked over and pointed his weapon at the wounded man's head. "That man is an enemy combatant who shot first, wounding my partner. We'd be dead if it wasn't for Blue. I have no problem putting a bullet through this man's head if his being injured is distracting you from saving my partner. In fact, I will do just that if you don't get over there and take care of Blue. If the dog doesn't survive, both of you may get a bullet to the brain pan. Understood?"

The doctor's eyes narrowed. Through gritted teeth he growled, "Yes."

As Cooper took off Blue's canine body armor, Harpole positioned herself so she could shoot any of the enemy soldiers if she had to. Once Blue was prepped, Cooper searched the planetary soldiers for weapons and took their helmets and body armor. A few had knives, but otherwise weren't concealing anything.

Cooper bound their wrists and ankles with strappers—pull-ties laced with metal. A prisoner would need an acetylene torch to cut through one. It would be easier to cut their hand off, but few people wanted freedom that badly.

Neither Cooper nor Harpole could hide their concern over the condition of their K-9 partner, but they tried, not wanting the doctor to realize he could turn things into another hostage situation.

The doctor reached for his utility belt and was greeted by two rifles clicking.

"The blast gave him multiple wounds. I need my surgical tools to get out the shrapnel."

"Just don't get any dumb ideas," Harpole said.

"Don't worry. I don't want a man's death on my conscience, so I'll save the dog."

Cooper leaned in, putting his mouth next to the corporal's ear. "Nice bluff by the way. A bullet would never set off Z-5."

Harpole smiled, knowing full well it would take an electric charge. Unfortunately, that included static discharge.

"Thank you. Yours too about shooting a wounded man. Now if you don't mind, I'm going to get to work if you think you can handle things here?"

Cooper nodded and took out his first aid kit. He went to the wounded planetary soldier and patched up the man so he could hold on long enough for the doctor to tend to him. Wilmer stopped his surgery on the dog long enough to look at Cooper and nod his thanks.

It took the better part of an hour, but the doctor managed to stitch up Blue. When he was done he took out an injector, an automated syringe, and placed it against the dog's side.

"Wait," Cooper said, but it was too late. He heard the hiss of the injection. "What did you give him?"

"Painkillers, antibiotics, and a sedative," the doctor said.

"We need him to find the rest of the explosives."

"He'll be in too much pain to be much use to you."

"How long will he be out?" Copper said.

"A few hours probably. I'm not a vet, but I estimated his weight and adjusted the dose accordingly." The doctor looked at his wounded comrade. "May I now help Jonesy?"

Cooper nodded and sat down next to Blue. With one hand he held his persuader rifle so he could fire on any of his prisoners or the doctor. He put the other hand in front of the dog's nose so he smelt that he was there.

Cooper, Harpole, and their prisoners all twitched at the sudden alarm, followed by the booming of several bunker doors slamming shut.

Harpole moved away from the bomb and put her sidearm along the doctor's temple. "What the hell's going on?"

"Somebody must've breached the children's area. I'm the only one coded genetically to be able to get in and out.

Anyone else goes through the doorway—even one of the kids—and this place goes into lockdown."

"You think one of the kids tried to get out?"

"Probably," Wilmer said, but Cooper's gut said he was lying.

"Are there any other soldiers here?"

Some of the men exchanged a glance.

"We are the only men here," Wilmer said.

Cooper looked over at where the Z-5 was. A timer counted down from one hour. "Corporal, I think we may be in trouble."

Harpole rushed to assess the situation, then cursed for quite some time. "It was set so if anyone tried to bypass security, it would blow everything. The countdown was probably to give the governor enough time to decide if he really wanted it to happen."

Harpole took out her radio.

Cooper grew nervous at the violation of protocol. "Regs say that we're not supposed to use any broadcast device in case explosives are on a detonator that would pick up the signal."

"We're locked in an armored bunker that is going to be lit up with Z-5 in an hour. We don't have a lot to lose here," Harpole said, lifting her radio to her mouth. "Boom Squad Alpha to Harpy Delta Seven." The corporal repeated the message several times, but no answer came. "Walls are too damn thick to get a signal out. We're on our own here. We really need Blue."

"That's not likely to happen," Cooper said, looking down at the drugged dog. He and Harpole turned to the doctor. "Can you wake him? Or do you know how to override the system to get the kids out?"

"No. I knew Cross was unbalanced, but I didn't know there were explosives. I'm here for one reason—to keep these children safe. My grandkids are among those taken and are here with the rest of the children. I wouldn't do anything to hurt any of them and I'd get them out if I could."

"Corporal, could we use some of the Z-5 to blow a hole?" Cooper asked.

"We could, but the way the bunker's built, the tunnel nearest the blast would be at risk of collapsing. And it makes no sense to leave without the children. Where are they, Doctor?"

The doctor wavered, looking at his patient.

"We all have less than an hour to live at this point. Jonesy will die with the rest of us. Do you think it's better to finish surgery on him now or later?" Cooper said.

Dr. Wilmer sighed. "I have most of the internal bleeding stopped. May I have one of the men apply pressure to the wound?"

Cooper nodded and the doctor pointed to one of the soldiers and showed him what to do, but Cooper left his strapper on.

"I'll show you where the children are and maybe together we can figure a way out," Wilmer said.

Cooper turned to the soldiers. "Listen up, gentlemen. You are on the honor system. Right now we are the only chance anyone has of getting out of here alive, yourselves and the children included. If we do not stop the timers on the explosives, we all die. Anyone who gets up or tries anything will be shot. If you're not here when it is time to leave, we will not come looking for you. When we evacuate, you will be left to be buried alive. That is, if you survive the blasts. If anyone touches one hair on Private Blue, I will personally put a bullet in his head. If Private Blue is missing or dead when we return, all of you will be left to die. Is everyone clear on the ground rules?"

Everyone nodded in acknowledgment.

"The children's quarters are this way," Dr. Wilmer said and lead them down a series of cement corridors.

Eventually they arrived at what had probably originally been intended to be a hanger or garage. The large area seemed small with the large number of children crammed into the space.

"How many?" Cooper said.

"Over two thousand. We've been running low on food and had to break out the emergency ration bars two days ago. Not very tasty, but one bar has enough nutrients for a day. The system recycles and purifies fluids with minimal loss."

The children appeared terrified by the wailing of the alarm, some of them huddling together in groups. The doctor waved to two girls who smiled and waved back. Cooper assumed they were his grandchildren.

"How do we talk to them?" Cooper said.

"Blue switch. Flip it and speak into the microphone," Wilmer said.

Cooper turned on the speaker system and cleared his throat. "Hello, children. I'm Sergeant Cooper and this is Corporal Harpole. We are with the 142$^{nd}$ Starborne and have come here to take you all home, once we take care of what is making the alarm go off. Please sit tight and we will be back shortly," he said, flipping the switch off. "At least I hope we will. Doctor, do you have any idea what other areas explosives might be in?"

"None. Why wouldn't there be just the one?"

"Structurally speaking, there needs to be at least one more set of explosives to bring this entire bunker down. Possibly more. In the other bunkers, we found at least three batches. Each of them was shielded from technological detection, which is why we needed Blue."

"So if Blue was back to normal, maybe you'd be able to defuse the bombs and we would be able to get the children out," Wilmer said.

"That was the plan, but we figured on having Blue and not having to beat the clock like this," Cooper said. "It doesn't matter, because Blue is no shape to help."

"What if I told you there was a way that he could be?" the doctor said.

"You got a magic wand?" Harpole said.

"The next best thing. We have a splicing chamber."

Harpole let out a whistle and a few colorful expressions. "You're telling me a backwater world like this has an SC?"

"We're not that backwater. The Host has splicer soldiers and set up chambers on different worlds to replenish their ranks. Do you have any in the 142$^{nd}$ Starborne?"

"None. Humans only, no monsters," Cooper said. "Major Benedict is big on that."

"How's a splicer going to help Blue? It's supposed to mix animal DNA with humans to get werewolves and other man-beasts," Harpole said.

"It has a reset button. They can sample unspliced DNA and reboot it," the doctor said.

"Then why isn't it used for dying people and fallen soldiers?" Cooper said.

"Because it's dangerous. Subjects sometimes die. And I've never heard of a case where a rebooted human subject came through with their memories intact."

"Then it's no dang good. Blue went through a lot of training, well over a year. We revert him back to a puppy and he'll have the talent, but not the ability," Cooper said, frowning. "What was Cross doing with it?"

"After the Host returned to Earth, he took control of almost everything they left behind. He announced everything would be safest with him. I believe he was planning on building up his forces with splicers," the doctor said, breaking eye contact. "I have another idea. We can mix your dog's DNA with one of you. You already have the knowledge and as a splicer you'd have the ability to sniff out the explosives."

"And live out the rest of our lives as a splicer freak? You've got to be kidding me. How about we do it to you?" Harpole said.

"First off, because if any of the children get injured, I'm the only doctor. Second, I have no idea how to do your jobs. You'd have to train me. You think we can do that in enough time to defuse the bombs?"

"No," Harpole said.

"I'll do it," Cooper said.

"Coop, are you nuts?" Harpole said.

"It's the only choice. We're willing to risk our lives to save these kids. It's part of the job. Why? Because we're soldiers. Nothing's changed. I do this and maybe two thousand kids live. Plus you and Blue. I don't, we all die. Doctor, does this machine have stored DNA?"

"No, the Host took that with them. You'd have to put Blue or at least a tissue sample in the extractor portion of the splicer."

"Doc, will it hurt either of them?" Harpole said.

"Blue, no. It will only be reading him. The sergeant, well

it's very likely. Rewriting DNA is painful."

"Then we are not turning you into a splicer freak. We'll find another way," Harpole said.

"Okay, so long as you can do it in the next thirty seconds, because that's about all the time we can spare. If you have another way out, trust me I'd be happy to do it."

Half a minute's worth of ticks counted off. Then Corporal Louise Harpole did a very uncharacteristic thing and authorized a single tear to roll down her face.

"Damn it, Coop. You outrank me. Order me to do it," she said.

"Not a chance. Doc, let's go."

They retrieved Blue and the doctor led them to a sealed room. Inside was the splicing chamber. It was a large metal tube with all sorts of energy emitters attached to it. Legend had it that it was originally designed for teleportation, but there was a fly in the ointment when the first person to try it wasn't the only living thing to go through. It ended messily, but the technology had been improved since. Cooper stripped down and got inside the tube. Anything extra on him could end up reconstituting inside of him. The doctor took a blood sample and put it in a small glass tube, then did the same for Blue. Instead of a teleport chamber, there was a scanning one. Harpole placed the still unconscious dog inside so he could be scanned fully. The doctor claimed the sampler could work around the wound and bandage.

"Sergeant Cooper, are you ready?" Wilmer asked.

"Get it done, Doctor," Cooper said.

Harpole leaned into the doctor's ear and whispered, "He dies and you won't make it until the bomb blast."

The doctor nodded and worked the controls like he had done it before. Harpole watched exactly what he did.

She was a quick learner. She had to be to survive in her profession.

Cooper screamed as the chamber filled with energy that lit up the room like the place had been filled with magnesium flares. The power drain dimmed the lights making the glow even more blinding. Then the screams stopped and Cooper was gone.

"Turn it off," Harpole said.

"It is too late. If we turn it off now, he won't reform. He'll just be dead. We just have to wait and pray," the doctor said.

Harpole thought it would take longer. From her perspective, it did. However, it was only a matter of minutes before the chamber returned to its inert state and the lights came back on. Harpole ran to the door and pulled it open. She caught her naked partner before he collapsed to the floor. "Coop, are you okay?"

Sergeant Cooper seemed to be taking stock of his own body. Slowly, he tested to see if his legs could still support him.

"I think I am. I feel stronger. My senses are sharper, like a flea on steroids with a telescope and a hearing aid set for eavesdropping."

"You still look like you," Harpole said. "And sound like you. I still don't know what you are talking about. I guess I was expecting you to be furrier."

The corporal had spoken too soon because Sergeant Cooper fell to his knees screaming as the hair on his body grew longer and thicker. The shape of his skull changed to something halfway between human and canine. His face elongated and his teeth grew larger, as did his ears. Cooper's hands twisted into a mix of hand and paw that ended in claws.

Harpole tightened her grip on her rifle. "Coop, are you in there?"

"I'm still me," said a voice that was still the sergeant's, yet animal. Cooper tried to pull on his uniform pants. The results were less than satisfactory. Not only had he grown larger and more muscular, but the shape of his legs and joints had changed. He was able to button them, but just barely and only due to the belt and waistband being adjustable.

"Give me the Z-5. I'll take a sniff then I'll start searching the place."

It took him a few moments to get used to his new body. He stumbled a few times and had to close his eyes more than once to get used to the new way the world looked. He didn't lose color vision so much as to have a new vision layer overlap everything. He could hear heartbeats and smell emotions. Once he had the basics sorted out, it didn't take long for Cooper to find the second batch of explosives in the soldiers' living quarters.

Cooper put his earpiece back on, although it didn't fit properly anymore. "This is all that's in this area. I'll search for the next batch. The radios should still work inside the bunker, so I'll call you when I find it. Doctor, you're with me."

A search of all the areas except the largest turned up nothing.

The doctor and sergeant stopped in front of the children's quarters and exchanged a look.

"How do we get inside?" Cooper said.

"It's simple. Plug in a code to the door and walk through. Someone already set off the alarms, so there's nothing to stop you."

"You're coming with me. I look pretty scary now and I

don't want to frighten the children, so it's your job to keep them calm while I search the place."

The doctor told him the code. Cooper hit the keypad and the door slid open.

"Doctor, you go first and prepare them. I'll be right behind you."

The doctor went through the doorway and pulled a wireless microphone from his pocket. He hit the button on the side and spoke. "Children, we have a man who is a splicer. He needs to search these quarters for something. Then he and his partner will be getting all of us out of here, so give him space and don't worry. Despite his appearance, he is a soldier. He won't hurt you."

As the man-dog came through, Cooper was surprised to see not so much panic as curiosity and wonder. The children had never seen a splicer and were far more intrigued than scared. He stopped short under the gaze of all those young eyes and found himself wanting to growl. Instead, he saluted, then got to work. He caught the faint scent of the explosive and followed it to the far end of the chamber where it was stronger. Cooper pulled off a panel and hit the side of his ear set comm. "Partner, I found the third explosive cache at the back of the children's chamber."

"I've got this one deactivated. I'm on my way."

As Harpole rounded the corner to the entrance to the children's chamber, she saw someone disappear around the corridor. "Freeze!"

The shadow kept running in the direction of the splice chamber.

"Sergeant, we have a hostile running loose in the compound. You want that I should pursue?"

"Negative, Corporal. Explosives are our first priority.

We'll track him down later. Who knows, I may be able to find him just like a bloodhound."

Cooper told her the entrance code.

"Doctor, who is that? You said there were no more soldiers."

"No, I said no more men."

"So it's a woman?"

"No."

"Doctor…"

"That is all I'm going to tell you."

"We will finish this later. For now, please get all the children away from here." Cooper's voice was almost a growl, although there was little hostility in his tone.

"Will moving save them if the Z-5 goes off?"

The dog soldier shook his head. "Detonators can explode too."

The doctor nodded and did as instructed.

By the time Harpole arrived, Cooper already had the wall taken apart.

Harpole got to work testing wires and circuits with her tools and goggles. Several minutes later, she turned and smiled. "All safe."

"But you did it wrong," Cooper said with what could now be easily described as a wolfish grin. Harpole cocked her head to the side. "You know you're not supposed to disarm the final one until the last ten seconds for dramatic effect. We had a good eleven minutes left."

"We defusers don't want more drama than we have to have. Are there any more explosives?"

"None that I can smell," Cooper said.

"Fine, then I'll try to hack open the doors. The only good thing about Cross tying the explosives into the bunker systems is we should be able to use my defuser pad to connect and end the lockdown. I can even tap into their comm system to contact Harpy Delta Seven and give them an update. Let them know that the splicer dog solider is a friendly."

Cooper nodded his canine head, then went over to the doctor. "The corporal is trying to get the doors open. However, someone is running around loose. I'm going to go check the prisoners. Doctor, you need to tell me right now, no more games—who else is in the compound?"

The doctor was torn between loyalty to the unit he served and to the people who had just saved the life of that unit and over two thousand children, some of them his own family. "Carlos Samsa was here before our group and the children arrived. It seems Cross may have started his own splicer soldier program already. Carlos is one of them and as such is not in my chain of command. He tends to keep to himself. I suspect he must be the one that set off the alarm. He's not the bravest man in the world despite his new advantages."

"Which are what exactly?" Cooper said.

Doctor Wilmer looked down at his feet and answered in a whisper. "Insect."

"What kind?"

"Cockroach. They stowed away with us from Earth and Cross figured it was the best choice for his select forces. There were a Baker's dozen made."

"Made by who?"

The doctor sighed. "Me. It was the price I paid to be in command here. I didn't want to do it, but I had no choice."

"We always have a choice, Doctor. It's just not always a pleasant one."

"Don't judge me. Not all soldiers are good men and I knew some of them might look upon the older girls as women. By being in command, I could protect the all the children."

"So we're dealing with thirteen roach splicers?" Cooper said, trying to keep panic from coloring his new voice.

"No. One died in the process. Five went mad soon after. Cross sent the others out to crush the rebels. Carlos Samsa stayed behind to guard the splice chamber."

"And you didn't think to mention this to us when we went there? Hoping we would be ambushed?" Cooper said, trying not to focus on the fact that almost half of the splicers lost their minds or wonder if or when it would happen to him.

"No. You were our only hope to survive. Carlos had deserted his post days ago. I assumed we would be safe."

"What about having him loose among the children? How would a bug man think of them?"

Wilmer looked defiantly at the dog soldier. "He knows I would kill him if he harmed any of them."

"And he is afraid of you?"

"No, but he believes me. And the other men do not like what he has become, and they have orders to kill him if he tries to hurt a child."

"Is he rational?" Cooper asked.

"As rational as he was before. Maybe less."

"I want you broadcasting on the speakers, asking Samsa to turn himself in. We won't harm him, only immobilize him like the other planetary soldiers. If he doesn't, we will hound him and hunt him down…."

Dr. Wilmer smirked. "Interesting choice of words." The doctor did as he was asked, but there was no response. Then the power dimmed.

"The same thing happened when you were in the splicing chamber," Harpole said.

"Blue!" Cooper said, already running before he finished shouting his partner's name. He stopped only to punch in the code to get through the door. Harpole followed right behind. Despite his new form, Cooper had not abandoned his weapons. The soldiers used standard procedure to enter the room, one covering the other. Blue was still unconscious and off to the side where they had left him, but the chamber was smoking as if it had just been used.

"Did he use the slice chamber again?" Harpole said. "And why?"

"We have to assume yes. And I have no idea. I don't see him anywhere in the room."

"That's because you didn't look hard enough." The voice came from the ceiling, a good twenty feet high. The 142$^{nd}$ Starborne soldiers lifted their persuaders toward the ceiling and were greeted with a sight that was more insect than human. Samsa opened fire on them with a sidearm. They both returned fire. Samsa crawled evasively while shooting back. Cooper moved so he shielded Blue. After emptying his weapon, Samsa scurried away.

"I swear I hit him," Harpole said.

"Judging from the smell, you did, but it didn't slow him down."

The splice chamber had cement blocks that went up to the ceiling, except for one section that was open for power conduits, but it left room enough for whatever it was they saw to get into the next section of the bunker.

"We have to go after him," Harpole said.

"But we can't leave Blue. The bug might come back."

Cooper took the uniform shirt that was still on the floor where he left it and fastened a makeshift sling for the injured dog, which he slung across his back.

"I'll go up and over, you go around," Cooper said.

"Need goggles?" Harpole said, putting hers on.

"I think I can see better without them now," Cooper said. With Blue on his back, Cooper scaled the twenty-foot wall quicker than he thought possible. His Host training had included scaling buildings and mountains, but he had never been this fast before.

The two soldiers came into the next chamber, one high and the other low, but there was no sign of the bug man. Together they moved to the next chamber. As they stepped inside, Cooper heard a faint click and pushed Harpole back into the corridor, shielding her and Blue as the room exploded.

When the ringing in his ears lessened, Cooper shouted, "Are you okay?"

Harpole nodded.

"Was that Z-5?"

"No. Gas, probably a tank from the kitchen. We need to squish this guy," Harpole said.

The soldiers cautiously moved down the hallway, which circled back around toward the main section of the bunker. They came to a place where the corridor split.

Cooper lifted his canine nose in the air. He sniffed both branches and chose the one on the right.

The soldiers exchanged a look of concern as the corridor led back to the children's chamber. Their worry was well-founded. As they rounded the corner, children were screaming and pouring out of the door of their gilded cage. The soldiers didn't bother with crowd control and instead went back inside.

The dog soldier got down on one knee and gently stopped one of the fleeing children. "What's going on?"

"There's a monster bug and it grabbed two of the kids. I think he's going to eat them," the child said.

"Don't worry. I'll find the bug man and get those kids away from him. Which way did he go?"

The child pointed and both soldiers rushed in that direction. They got to the far end of the children's chamber, where the doctor was trying to reason with the insect splicer, who was holding one of the doctor's grandchildren on either side of him.

"Let them go and take me instead," Dr. Wilmer said.

"Nope." His voice sounded like air forced through a metal grate. "You might cause trouble. They'll behave if they know what's good for them."

"Carlos, you don't want to do this. Our job is to protect these children, not put them in danger."

"That's your job, Doc. Mine was to protect the splice chamber and you let outsiders in and made one of them into a splicer. Cross will have your head."

"Cross is dead. He lined this place with explosives and you set off the timer when you came in here the first time."

Samsa shrugged. "Figured the Host wouldn't be shooting up the kiddies and I wanted to last long enough to offer them my services." The roach soldier turned to see Copper and Harploe coming toward him from different points. "Damn. I figured my little bomb would kill you two. Since I fired up the splicing chamber as bait to get you both into my little deathtrap, the Host is probably not going to welcome me with open arms. Look, I just want out of here, but if you try to take me out first, I got shields."

"We're not going to try and take you out," Cooper said, his persuader pointed at the roach man's head. The dog soldier was not sure how well his motor memory carried over to his new body and didn't want to risk a shot.

"Tell that to Jonesy, dog man."

"Jonesy fired on us first. We were protecting ourselves. Why don't you put down those kids and we can talk about this like civilized men," Cooper said as Harpole moved to flank the insect splicer.

"Have you looked in the mirror lately? Neither one of us is a man any longer. How about you just let me go?"

"Okay," Cooper said.

"What do you mean okay?" Samsa hissed. At the horrifying sound, the two girls the insect soldier held started sobbing, then tried to stop, their eyes darting at the bug man's face, their bodies trembling. It was a valiant, but ultimately doomed effort and they started crying again.

"I'll let you go if you let the kids go. Easy solution. Everybody wins and nobody gets hurt," Cooper said.

"You mean you'll let me walk right out of the bunker?" the roach man said. His face had been warped by the insect DNA, which made his expressions hard to read, but Cooper's best guess was that it was one of disbelief.

"My mission is to save the kids. You haven't hurt any of them, so I have no reason to stop you. If you were to hurt them, my view on that would change."

The roach soldier nodded. "We're still locked in."

"No. I hacked the doors. We can out get out," Harpole said.

"So how about we head to the door together?" Cooper said.

"All right. Leave your guns with your partner there and

then we'll walk out to the bunker exit. I let the kids go there and I'll leave."

"I can do that." Cooper took off his persuader rifle and his sidearm and handed both of them to his corporal. He tapped his earpiece and used the hand signal for "report." Harpole nodded understanding, but her eyes looked at him as if he were crazy.

Cooper tried to hand Blue off.

"Leave the dog where he is. It'll slow you down and make you think twice about doing something stupid because he'll be the first one hurt," Samsa said. "Now how do I know this isn't some sort of trick?"

"Because I give you my word as a member of the 142nd Starborne that I will let you walk out of this bunker, provided you give the children to me unharmed before you leave. That and what other choice do you have?"

The roach soldier nodded and Cooper led the way to the exit, holding his hands above his shoulders. He could hear the children's rapid heartbeats and smell their fear and tears. One had even peed. It was disconcerting, to say the least. Samsa, on the other hand, smelled of some odd amalgam of clean and decay. Cooper could still smell whatever passed for blood in him, but the bullet wounds had already closed over and healed. He failed to understand the desperate logic that convinced Samsa that it was better to live on as a bug than to die as a man. What could Cross have promised him to entice him to give up his humanity?

When they got to the exit, Cooper did a quick count of the tied and bound soldiers. They were all still there, even the one applying pressure to the wounded soldier. They looked at Cooper and Samsa with a mix of fear and disgust.

Sergeant Cooper hit the open switch and the bunker

door whooshed open, the sunlight almost blinding in comparison to the bunker's low-level lights.

Samsa backed his way up to the door and dropped the children. They stumbled, then ran to Cooper. He knelt and wrapped a furry arm around each of them. "You're okay. You both did very good and were very brave. I'm proud of you. Now go back to Corporal Harpole and she'll take care of you. And send your grandpa to take care of Jonesy."

Cooper turned to watch the girls run down the corridor and found he had an instinct to race after them but was able to suppress it with a little difficulty. Unfortunately, during the time his eyes were following the children, Samsa came at him, the roach man throwing the dog soldier against the wall. Copper turned and took the blow on his shoulder rather than hurt Blue. The dog soldier barely got his arms up in time to catch the roach man's two human arms from grabbing Blue, but Samsa also had four smaller stubs growing out of his sides, each one of them with hands and fingers. This wasn't hand-to-hand, but many-hand-to-hand combat.

"I don't trust you to not try and put a bullet in my head. Not that more bullets would hurt me much now, but why take the chance?" Samsa hissed.

The bug man was larger and stronger and pinned the dog soldier. Cooper couldn't get better leverage without risking Blue being crushed.

Cooper's knees started to give. Much more and he'd be on the floor. He growled his frustration and another voice took up the song.

The pressure from the insect hands suddenly lessened as the growling from the vicinity of Cooper's waist got louder. The dog soldier looked down in time to see Blue's jaws snap shut around the roach man's groin. All of Samsa's arms went limp as he crumbled over in pain.

*"I guess the splicing didn't get rid of all of the man,"* Cooper thought wryly, trying to suppress a grin. Blue let go and Cooper very gently set the dog on the floor.

Blue growled at Samsa. Cooper dropped into a defensive position, ready to attack. Samsa looked from one to the other, then chose the better part of valor and scurried out of the bunker and into the sights of about fifty soldiers of the 142nd Starborne.

A voice ordered him to freeze, but the roach man ignored the order. Cooper looked outside as bullets riddled the insect body. It was enough to make Samsa stumble but not fall. However, a grenade launcher reduced him to so much goo. It was as if a giant exploding boot had smashed him from above.

Cooper put the dog down and got on one knee. "Thanks, boy, but this could get messy. Safest if you just stay here."

Cooper touched his earpiece. "This is Sergeant Cooper. I assume you got Corporal Harpole's report. My appearance is now a bit unusual, but I'm a friendly. Do not open fire. Repeat—do not open fire."

"Roger that, Sergeant Cooper."

Dartanian Cooper slowly walked out of the bunker, his hands open and out to his sides. Blue ignored his orders, and protectively limped along beside him. There were fifty armed soldiers, but Cooper was happy to see that not one of them trained their weapons on them. However, he also noted that not many fingers were that far away from the trigger. Cooper sighed because he realized in their place, he would be doing the same thing.

He was a little surprised to see who came out to greet

him.

Cooper gave a quick salute. "Major Benedict, sir."

It was unusual for a major to hold command over those with much higher ranks, but the 142$^{nd}$ had adapted to it. Benedict returned the salute. "Sergeant Cooper, the mission was successful?"

"Yes, sir. All the children are safe. Soldier Samsa there not so much…"

"Samsa? That was really the name of the bug splicer?" Benedict said with a grin. "Was his first name Gregor?"

"It was Carlos, but I'm not sure why that is amusing."

"Not a big fan of 19th-century literature, I take it?"

"No, sir. These days I don't get to read much except for explosive and bomb technical manuals."

"Understandable. We've already encountered one of the other bug splicers and we'll have to locate the other five. Finish your status report, Sergeant."

"The planetary forces have a wounded soldier, otherwise no casualties. He needs more medical care. Their doctor was helpful in assisting us. All two thousand children appear to be safe and Corporal Harpole has disarmed all the explosives."

"Excellent work. Harpole's report was very brief, but am I to understand that you willingly spliced yourself together with DNA from Blue?"

"Yes, sir. Blue was wounded protecting Corporal Harpole and myself and was unable to complete the mission. The children's lives were in jeopardy. We had little time to come up with a plan. This is the only way I could see to finish the mission. The planetary governor had booby-trapped the place. Within an hour, we and all civilians and enemy combatants would've been buried beneath the rubble."

Hans Benedict met Cooper's eyes unflinchingly. "You are aware that there is no known method to reverse a splicing?"

"Yes, sir. I knew that before I did it. I also know your opinion on monster soldiers, sir. If need be, I can retire from active duty."

"Nonsense. It is true that I have issues with some of those the Host had chosen to employ as soldiers, but I see no monster here. Only a hero." Major Benedict stuck out his hand. It took the canine Sergeant Cooper a moment to realize what he was doing and return the handshake. "Excellent, selfless work. Congratulations on a successful mission, Captain Cooper."

"Sir, I'm only a sergeant."

Benedict smiled. "Not anymore. With the fall of Earth, the 142nd needs all the brave and selfless officers we can get and I'm not above jumping a qualified candidate a few ranks. You just proved yourself one of that number." Benedict bent down on one knee and extended his hand to Blue. The dog returned the shake, then whimpered at the pain the movement caused him. "Medic, we need a stretcher over here now for Private Blue."

Two medics came over and gently put the dog on a stretcher. Blue lay down.

"It's okay, boy. Rest," Cooper said and Blue fell asleep almost instantly.

Major Benedict placed his hand on top of the dog's head and petted it gently. "Good job, soldier," he whispered.

"What's going to happen to Blue, sir?"

"We'll make sure he's patched up as best we can. If he's able, he'll return to active duty with you. If he's not, he shall continue to live with you. A soldier wounded in the line of duty deserves the right to grow old with his family. We owe him that much. And perhaps stud him out to father his own replacements."

Cooper smiled. "I think Blue might be hoping for retirement just because of that option, sir."

"Wouldn't we all? And I suppose there is no reason he can't do both. Do you feel fit to help with the evacuation of the children and their return to their families?"

"Yes sir, but what about my appearance? It might frighten some of the families."

"It might, but we'll let those same people know that you and your partners saved their children. I think that will go a long way toward helping them get over their prejudice. If any of them you any grief, I will talk to them personally. That goes for anyone, planetside or shipside."

Cooper snapped off another salute. "Yes, sir. Thank you, sir."

Benedict again returned the salute. "No, Captain Cooper, thank you."

The major made a mental note to arrange for counseling and monitoring of Captain Cooper. Splicer soldiers were phenomenal in battle, but more than half of them eventually took on the instincts of the animal they shared DNA with and had to be put down, often by way of suicide missions.

Cooper was thinking along similar lines, only with a great deal more worry. The only thought keeping him from panicking was that his spliced DNA came from Blue, a dog willing to die to protect his human partners. A dog that was braver and more loyal than a great many people. Cooper couldn't see how having those parts of Blue inside of him would make him go mad. In fact, it might end up making him a better human.

There has long been a debate among certain obscure and drunken literary scholars about whether **PATRICK THOMAS** was raised by Cthulhu, a leprechaun in a Manhattan bar, or two human parents. What there is no arguing about is that Patrick is the award-winning author of 40 books including the beloved fantasy humor *Murphy's Lore series* (9 books from *Tales from Bulfinche's Pub* to *The Mug Life*), as well as 2 books in the future space adventures in the *Startenders* series.

The Murphy's Lore After Hours spin-offs star the half pixie/ogre Terrorbelle (*Fairy With A Gun, Fairy Rides The Lightning,* and *Terrorbelle The Unconquered*); the former demon-possessed serial killer Agent Karver of the Department of Mystic Affairs (*Dead To Rites, Rites of Passage*); the cursed magí Hex (*By Darkness Cursed* and *By Invocation Only*); Vince Argus, the Soul For Hire (*Greatest Hits*); and Negral, a forgotten Sumerian god who works as Hell's Detective (*Lore & Dysorder, Bullets & Brimstone,* and the graphic novel *The Moon Maniac* with Blair Webb).

His *Mystic Investigators* paranormal mystery series includes *Shadows & Brimstone* (omnibus of *Bullets & Brimstone* and *From The Shadows* with John L. French), *Once Upon In Crime* (omnibus of *Once More Upon A Time* and *Partners In Crime* with Diane Raetz) *Mystic Investigators,* and *Mean Streets. Assassins' Ball* is his first traditional mystery, co-written with John L. French. He co-edited *Camelot 13, New Blood, Hear Them Roar* and was an editor for the magazines *Fantastic Stories of the Imagination* and *Pirate Writings.*

His other works include the steampunk *As The Gears Turn.* the space epic *Exile & Entrance*, and the *Bikini Jones* series. Patrick's darkly humorous advice column *Dear Cthulhu* has been running since 2005 and has 6 collections including *Cthulhu Knows Best* and *What Would Cthulhu Do?* The Dear Cthulhu advice empire has expanded from magazines and books to radio as Dear Cthulhu now broadcasts monthly on the show Destinies: The Voice of Science Fiction which is hosted by Dr. Howard Margolin.

Over 100 of his stories have been published in magazines and anthologies. His noir novella appears in *Murder in Montague Falls*. A number of his books were part of the props department of the *CSI* television show and *Nightcaps* was even thrown at a suspect's head. His urban fantasy *Fairy With A Gun* had been optioned for film and TV by Laurence Fishburne's Cinema Gypsy Productions. Top Men Productions has turned his *Soul For Hire* Story, *Act of Contrition*, into a short film.

He also writes books for kids as PATRICK T. FIBBS including the YA *Emotional Support Nifghtmare*, the midde readers U*ndead Kid Diaries: Over My Dead Body, the Babe B. Bear Mysteries: Bad Hair Day, Joy Reaper Checks Out,* the picture book *Fushcia The Mermaid Who Loved Pink*, and *the Ughabooz* picture books *5 Silly Monsters Jumping On The Zed* and *On Top Of A Yeti*, and the early reader *Soggy Goes to the Beach.*

Please drop by www.patthomas.net or follow him at I_PatrickThomas at Twitter or www.facebook.com/PatrickThomasAuthor to learn more.

MYSTIC INVESTIGATORS
BY
PATRICK THOMAS
A MYSTIC INVESTIGATORS OMNI
SHADOW & BRIMSTON
From the authors of Assassin's Ball and Rites of Passage
PATRICK THOMAS & JOHN L. FRENCH
A MYSTIC INVESTIGATORS BOOK
MEAN STREETS
From the Author of Fairy With A Gun and Lore & Dysorder
PATRICK THOMAS
A MYSTIC INVESTIGATORS
ONCE UPON IN CRIM
From the creators of the Wildsidhe Chronicles
PATRICK THOMAS & DIANE RAETZ
DOWN THESE
MEANS STREETS
of Magic & Monsters walk the
MYSTIC INVESTIGATOR

## Being *CURSED* to wear a bikini
## Won't stop this Hero
## From *SAVING* the world

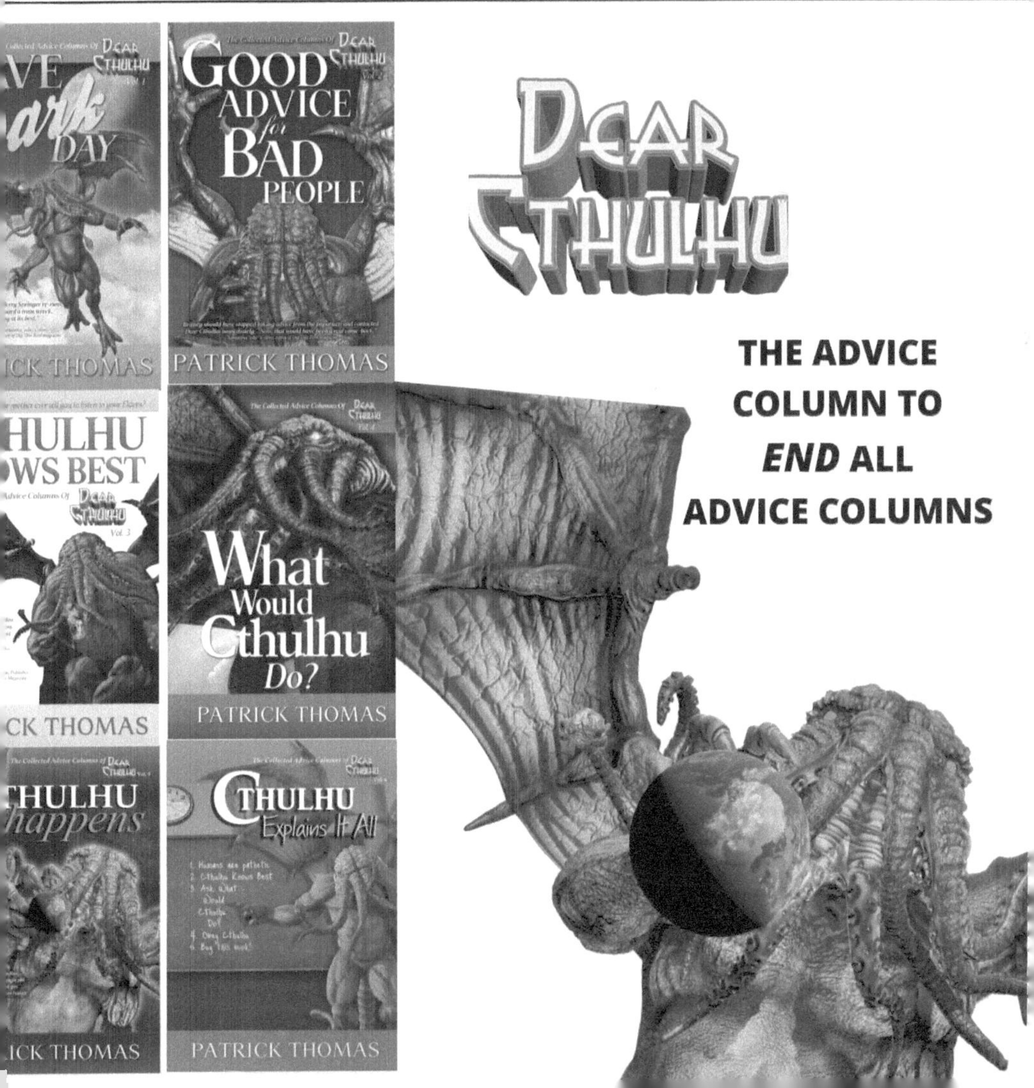

# Dear Cthulhu

## THE ADVICE
## COLUMN TO
## *END* ALL
## ADVICE COLUMNS

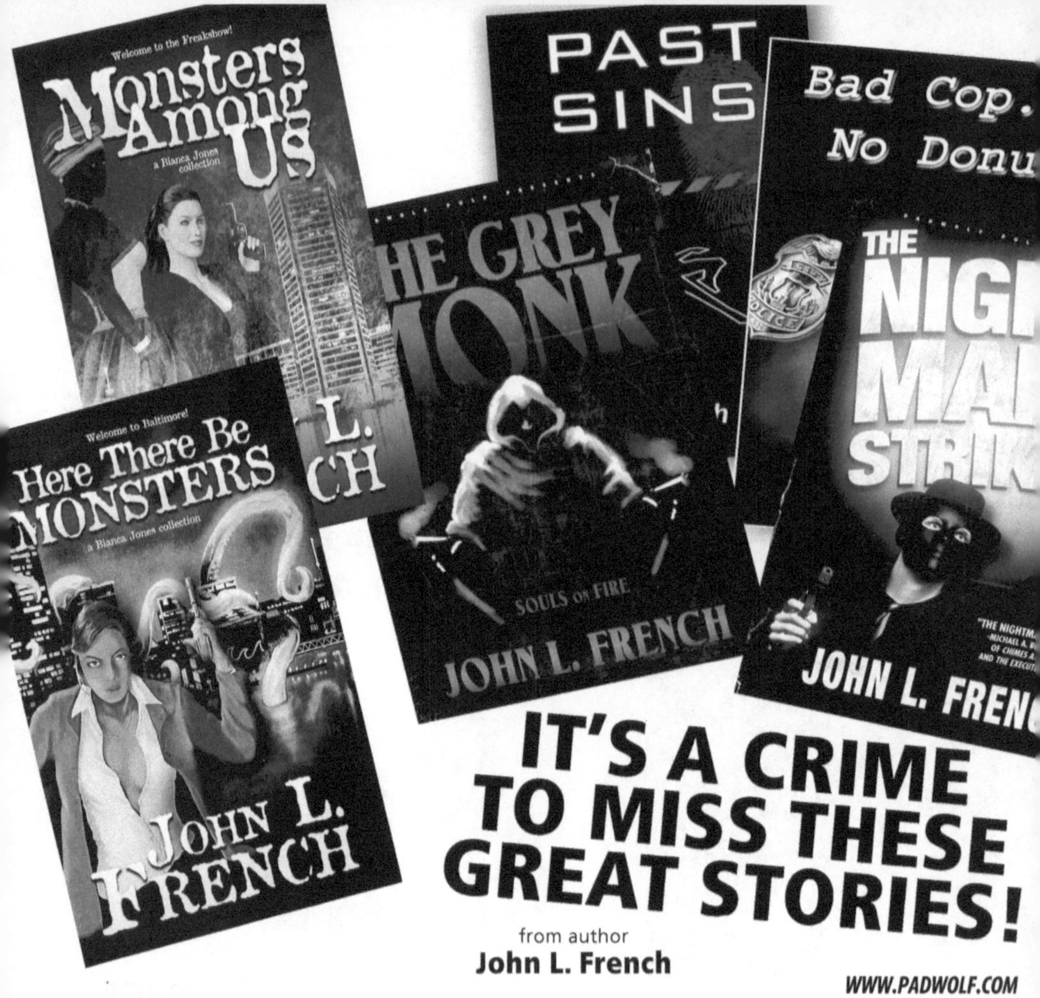
Welcome to the Freakshow!
Monsters Among Us
a Bianca Jones collection
PAST SINS
Bad Cop.
THE GREY MONK
SOULS ON FIRE
JOHN L. FRENCH
Welcome to Baltimore!
Here There Be MONSTERS
a Bianca Jones collection
JOHN L. FRENCH
JOHN L. FRENC
IT'S A CRIME TO MISS THESE GREAT STORIES!
from author
John L. French
WWW.PADWOLF.COM

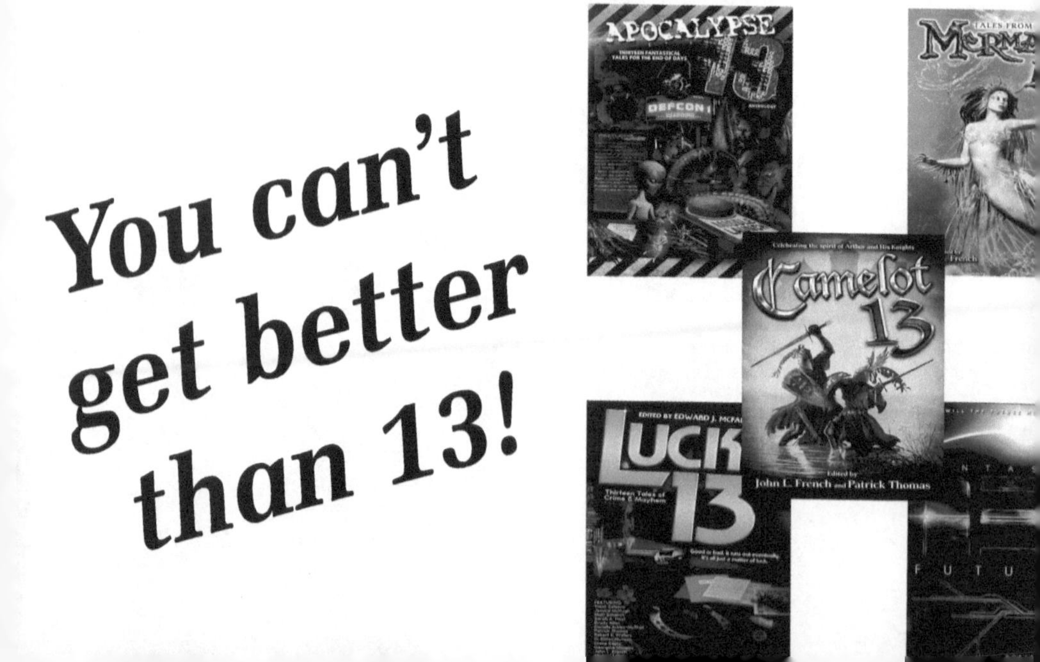
You can't get better than 13!
APOCALYPSE 13
Celebrating the spirit of Arthur and His Knights
Camelot 13
Edited by
John L. French and Patrick Thomas
LUCK 13
Thirteen Tales of Crime & Mayhem

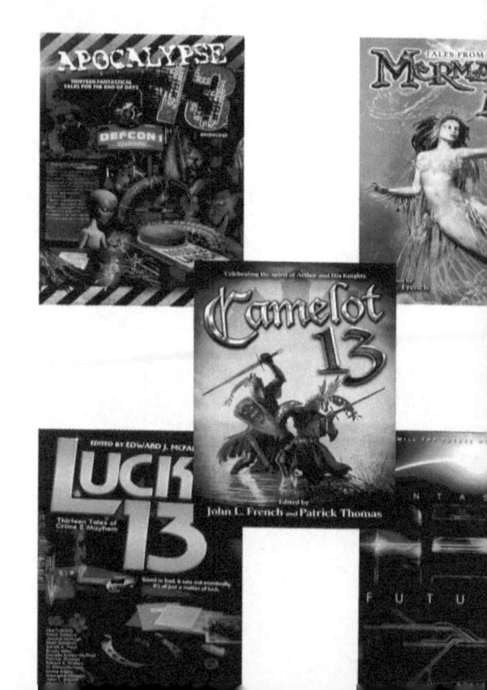